William Richard Hughes

Constance Naden

A Memoir

William Richard Hughes

Constance Naden
A Memoir

ISBN/EAN: 9783337380243

Printed in Europe, USA, Canada, Australia, Japan

Cover: Foto ©Raphael Reischuk / pixelio.de

More available books at **www.hansebooks.com**

CONSTANCE NADEN:

A MEMOIR.

BY

WILLIAM R. HUGHES, F.L.S.,

LATE PRESIDENT OF THE BIRMINGHAM NATURAL HISTORY AND MICROSCOPICAL
SOCIETY.

WITH AN INTRODUCTION

BY

PROFESSOR LAPWORTH, LL.D., F.R.S.,

AND ADDITIONS

BY

PROFESSOR TILDEN, D.Sc., F.R.S.,

AND

ROBERT LEWINS. M.D.,

ARMY MEDICAL DEPARTMENT.

London:
BICKERS & SON.

Birmingham:
CORNISH BROTHERS.
1890.

Es glühte *ihre* Wange roth und röther
Von jener Jugend die uns nie verfliegt,
Von jenem Muth, der früher oder später
Den Widerstand der stumpfen Welt besiegt;
Von jenem Glauben, der sich stets erhöh'ter,
Bald kühn hervor drängt, bald geduldig schmiegt,
Damit das Gute wirke, wachse, fromme!
Damit der Tag des Edlen endlich komme.—GOETHE.

CONTENTS.

PRINTED BY WRIGHT, DAIN, PEYTON, AND CO.,

AT THE HERALD PRESS, BIRMINGHAM.

INTRODUCTION.

INTRODUCTION.

The ground-work of this volume is a reprint of three articles which appeared in the pages of the *Midland Naturalist* during the months of April, May, and June, 1890. The larger section (Parts I. and II.) has been contributed by Mr. W. R. Hughes, F.L.S., a friend and admirer of Miss Naden, and one who was intimately associated with her during the last six years of her life, in a Society which has for its object the study and promulgation of Mr. Herbert Spencer's system of Synthetic Philosophy.

In his memoir Mr. Hughes endeavours to give a general view of the life of Miss Naden from her earliest years, and many of the links which go to make up the complete chain of facts were obtained by him from her personal friends and associates. In the present reprint the memoir has been greatly amplified, and several paragraphs—in consequence of additional information—have been introduced, and others partly rewritten.

The remaining section (Parts III. and IV.) has not been materially altered. Part III. was contributed by one of Miss Naden's friends and teachers, my colleague, Professor W. A. Tilden, F.R.S. Part IV. is the work of Dr. Robert Lewins, Miss Naden's life-long friend and philosophical mentor, to whose loving and generous regard for the memory of his former friend and pupil the public owe the publication of Miss Naden's posthumous works, and the Mason College the institution of the Constance Naden Medal, and the gift of a marble bust for its Library.

As no other memoir is likely to appear— at all events in a separate form—it is thought that the friends and admirers of Miss Naden would like to possess this little souvenir.

My own share in the symposium has been confined to penning these few lines of introduction; my friend, Dr. Lewins, having asked me to preface this little work with some words of my own.

I fulfil his kindly request with some reluctance and no little pain. Miss Constance Naden was, of all my geological pupils, from the first not so much a student, as an interested and sympathetic fellow-worker, and in her early death I have lost one of the best and dearest of my personal friends. I was acquainted with her some time before she joined my department in 1884, but it was during her attendance at my classes—from 1884 to 1887—that I slowly grew to recognise what a rich and well-balanced mind my pupil possessed. Thrown repeatedly together as we were in class, in the laboratory, and in frequent excursions, I learnt perhaps as much from her as she gained from me, and felt constantly that intellectual stimulus which always arises from association with the highest minds.

In her geological work Miss Naden shunned none of the so-called drier details, but went as earnestly, as steadily, and as carefully through them all as the student whose future wholly depends upon his accurate knowledge. But while she grasped and easily retained the facts of geology, I soon recognised that it was in reality the principles and the far-reaching conclusions of the science which attracted her—the awful immensity of past time—the slow but irresistible effects of natural causes—the gradual evolution of the geography of the globe—the upward sweep and elaboration of organic forms. In the quiet marshalling of hard facts and in rigid inference therefrom, she seemed to be in her natural element. There was never any need to point out to her a deduction: she made it in her own mind directly the premises were stated. Between the settled and the unsettled—the established and the disputed—regions in our science, she at once made instinctive separation. At the same time her sympathetic nature gave her a deep interest in those ambiguous and doubtful points where knowledge is small and authority great, points which exasperate and worry the ordinary student anxious to get on. In the past history and struggles of the science she was especially interested, and before her studies in geology came to an end, the science could claim her, if not as a devotee, yet certainly as one who knew and understood its facts and its principles, and had a deep and hearty sympathy with its methods and its conclusions.

But it was always perfectly clear to my mind that Miss Naden studied geology mainly as a source of actual knowledge, and as a means of mental culture. I never expected that she would become an original worker. But poet and philosopher as she was, the science was more or less a necessity to her. It gave her that infinitude of past time, in which she could trace for herself the numberless relationships which bind man to the earth and to his fellow-creatures, organic and inorganic ; and it spread out before her mind's eye that limitless theatre of evolution, in which she could watch for herself the forging of the great chain of life, of which man is the final and the crowning link.

For I take it, distinctly, that Miss Naden's study of geology, as that of other sciences, was only as a means to an end. She was above all things a student of man and of mind. But she wished to know all that was known, not that which was asserted or believed : to get down to the solid facts themselves, and to draw her own conclusions for herself alone. Her love of a fact, her horror of an opinion, was a bye-word amongst us. The old question—Man, whence and whither?—had for her the old irresistible fascination, and she came to science and not to authority for the answer. Whether that be the wrong or the right path, let others decide ; but one thing was always clear—her love of absolute truth, of uprightness of mind, of goodness of heart, and of all that makes for nobleness of soul, was as natural to her as the air she breathed.

Her studies never seemed to be in any sense laborious to her. She enjoyed her work, and found it interesting and natural, and therefore easy. In fact, I used frequently to tell her that she never studied at all, in the accepted sense of the word, and I doubt if—while I knew her— she ever did. She listened, she read, she selected, and she assimilated ; and the new ideas, the novel views, grew to be her own. In this way the range of her knowledge, the breadth of her views, and the originality of her

conceptions, gave a freshness, and an unexpected-
ness to her conversation, that endowed it with a
curious fascination. To the listener unfamiliar
with her training, her knowledge seemed to be,
what it really had become, a part of herself: as
in the case of her own Clarice,

"As though what others con with aching head
  This maiden knew by right inherited."

Scientific as was the bent of Miss Naden's
mind, and absorbed as she always was, more or
less, in scientific and literary work, there was
nothing of the sexless " blue stocking" about
her. She was always womanly, with many of
the instinctive proclivities, and all the tender
sympathies of her sex. Keen to see the foibles
and peculiarities of her associates, she had an
arch and quiet mode of ridiculing them in
confidential moments, which was exceedingly
comical and captivating. It was never malicious,
but filled with the pure girlish spirit of fun and
playfulness. Into the loves and sorrows of her
own personal friends she entered with the deepest
ardour, and it was a standing joke between her
and my wife, that, of all women, Constance
Naden was the most romantic.

Her love of art was almost as great as her
love of poetry ; and her knowledge of the great
painters and their individualities, deep and
thorough. A walk with her through a good

picture gallery was delightful. But it was more in the direction of form than of color that her sympathies tended. Sculpture, perhaps, even more than painting, attracted her fancy.

Of music she knew little or nothing. She often told me that neither melody nor harmony had the slightest power to move her, and that she recognised no distinction worth mentioning between the mental effects of the discordant strains of a German band and Hallé's masterly interpretation of one of the sonatas of Beethoven. But the innate appreciation of those delicate gradations of tone, of colour, of form and feeling, proper to the gifted musician, was just as unquestionably hers; though shown in a somewhat different direction. No one could listen to her conversation without frankly acknowledging the fact. And it was equally apparent in her exquisite appreciation of the delicacies of literary form and style, as evidenced in her own literary work—her papers and her poems.

But excellent as is Miss Naden's poetry, I doubt greatly whether she ever regarded poetry as the serious business of her life. It may be that she misunderstood her vocation, and that had she lived she would have stood in the first rank of our British poets. But with all her love for poetry, as being the noblest form of literature, and the highest medium for the

expression of the emotions ; her natural clear-
sightedness, and the scientific set of her mind,
intensified as they were by her later training,
led her, I suspect, to accord to it a secondary
place in her regard, because of its natural
tendency to substitute phrases for things, the
fascination of beauty for the dignity of truth.
Certainly, for many years past, her great aim
was to become, not a poet, but a student in
philosophy, a teacher of ethics.   Poetry had
gradually become to her more or less a
recreation.   " Clarice," she told me, was written
during her convalescence, after a sharp attack
of illness, in 1886, and other poems in similar
hours of enforced leisure, when real work, as she
termed it, was impossible.   Had she lived, it
would have been in the direction of philosophical
research—of the evolution of mind—that she
hoped to make her mark.   All her self-training
was directed instinctively to this end.   It was to
her mind the goal of the sciences, the lodestar
of poetry.   How much philosophy and literature
have lost in her early death we now can never
know.

She was, I think, at her best, in a quiet
evening spent in the society of her intimate and
sympathetic friends.   My wife and myself have
vivid recollections of her on many such occasions.
Leaning in her chair, with her fine head thrown

back in a characteristic attitude, she joined in the give and take of the conversation with quiet but deep enthusiasm. Never monopolizing the talk, she generally took, however, the largest share. She wandered on easily from grave to gay, from serious to sentimental : now discussing the latest scientific discovery—now reciting some fine passage from the poets—now deep in some philosophical theory—now laughing over the comical idiosyncrasies of some great authority— now telling, with sweet sympathy and dewy eyes, of the loves and sorrows of her friends. Poet, student, philosopher as she was, she was ever a true and tender-hearted woman ; and those who knew her best, only know how staunch, how dear a friend they have lost in Constance Woodhill Naden.

That the originality implied in the poems and scientific papers of Miss Naden, the work needed for that self-culture which was incessant, and the stress of self-repression that grew more or less habitual with her, should all entail a constant strain, too great for mind and body to bear without danger, is certainly probable. But that she was fully aware of the existence of such a strain herself, I doubt very much. She was distinctly an enthusiast in all she did, but she gave one the impression of being a quiet enthusiast, holding herself in easy and complete

control. I never saw her look wearied or
exhausted during the whole of her College
career. She always seemed to work, as I have
said, far less than other students, and yet to
accomplish more, and to be always ready and
fresh for some intellectual novelty, How much
of this was real, and how much due to her
instinctive habit of self-repression, it is impossible
to say.

But the change after her return from India
was great. She left us in youthful health and
strength. She returned a confirmed invalid.

Mr. Spencer, in his kindly and appreciative
letter, printed in the Appendix, suggests, indeed,
that Miss Naden's remarkable mental powers
" were developed at a physiological cost, which
her feminine organization was unable to bear."
It may be so. But she gave no evidence of this
while she was at College, nor do I imagine that
she would herself have acknowledged that this
was the case, even at the last. A few weeks
before her death she spent some hours with me
among the Natural History Collections and in
the Art Galleries of South Kensington. Bright
and sparkling as ever—keenly interested in all
the old work and the new opinions—her
enthusiastic and powerful mind over-mastered
her weakly frame, and to a stranger she must
have appeared refreshingly young and blooming

beside those pale, spectacle-eyed enthusiasts who occasionally wander through these neglected shades. It was the last time I saw her. Less than a month later that eager soul was stilled in death, the exhausted frame resting for ever

"In utter silence and in perfect peace."

CHAS. LAPWORTH.

MEMOIR.

I.

" Not less swift souls that yearn for light,
  Rapt after Heaven's starry flight,
  Would sweep the tracts of day and night."

The Two Voices, TENNYSON.

———

Miss Naden is dead! Such were the sorrowful words spoken with bated breath, and sympathetically passed on by the circle of intimate friends who received them about mid-day on Tuesday, the 24th of December, 1889, with a feeling akin to that hoping against hope which mortals are prone to cling to, peradventure they might by any possibility be afterwards contradicted. Alas! they were but too true, for their verification appeared in the evening journals,

" And sadly fell our Christmas-eve,"

as we realised the full force of the sudden and un-expected blow that had deprived the world of a fine and original thinker, Birmingham of its most gifted daughter, progressive Science of a most distinguished worker, and the writer of these lines of a warmly attached friend.

It is an exceptionally rare privilege to record the higher intellectual, and especially the philosophical, achievements of women, although our present

B

educational system—in which, thanks largely to the influence of Mr. Herbert Spencer's world-renowned work on education, and to the persistent and devoted labours of Professor Huxley, science has now a place— will doubtless develop more numerous instances in the future; but those who were privileged to know and understand Constance Naden and her aims and writings and powers best, presaged for her a future equal to George Eliot herself. A comparison, however, between the two Warwickshire ladies is scarcely possible—the latter died at the matured age of sixty-one, having completed her work—the former at the early age of thirty-one, having scarcely begun it. Miss Naden had certainly the advantage of a much better education, as well as a juniority of thirty years, which count largely on the raised plane of intellectual thought; and she gave substantial evidence in the good work which she left behind her of even better that might have been forthcoming in the future. The late Mr. Bray, of Coventry, who knew both ladies, was an immense admirer of Miss Naden. He considered her genius quite equal to that of George Eliot, and he told a mutual friend that he regularly read her "Pantheist's Song of Immortality" as his Sunday morning's Psalm. One point is very interesting to record :—the early Evangelical training of both ladies was somewhat similar, and they both subsequently exchanged the old for the new stand-point.

The cause of evolution has suffered severely by her premature dissolution, for she brought to bear on

its promulgation, not only a woman's sympathy and
a poet's instinct, but also a philosopher's acumen.
And now, indeed just at the commencement of her
literary career, and enriched as she was with the rare
combinations of genius, will, leisure, and ample means,
one of its ablest and most devoted exponents is
abruptly silenced for ever!

It is impossible within the brief limits of space
of this *con amore*, but otherwise inadequate memoir, to
do full justice to the merits of such a many-sided and
beautiful character. It is also not too much to say
that no woman of the century, or indeed of any
century, was better educated than Miss Naden—and
to prevent misconception I use the word educated in
the largest sense, as defined by Mr. Herbert Spencer
—and as will hereafter be shown from her versatility
of genius and talent, with a mind corrected and enlarged
by travel, no woman at her age ever gave such
abundant promise of brilliant and successful fruition.

The writer's experience of his lost and highly
valued friend only extended from the spring of 1884,
during the time of her later studentship at the Mason
College, and subsequently until the end came in 1889 ;
but a few details of her early school life—and later
student life—have been supplied from several trust-
worthy sources ; and such particulars relating to her
collegiate career, from a professorial point of view, as
are of public interest, have been most kindly and
sympathetically written by Professor Tilden, D.Sc.,
F.R.S., Professor of Chemistry at the college, who was
one of her teachers. Dr. Lewins has also contributed

a very valuable chapter containing an exposition of her hylo-idealistic standpoint as a supplement to this memoir.

Constance Caroline Woodhill Naden was born at No. 15, Francis Road (formerly Francis Street), Edgbaston, the West-End suburb of Birmingham, January 24th, 1858, and was the only child of Mr. Thomas Naden, the present President of the Birmingham Architectural Association, and Caroline Anne, only daughter by his second wife (Miss Field) of Mr. J. C. Woodhill, Pakenham House, Charlotte Road, Edgbaston. Mrs. Naden died on the 5th of February following, and it is touchingly recorded that when the final parting came between her mother and the young wife, the latter said, "You will have baby!" That sacred trust was at once acknowledged and faithfully kept, for the little infant was taken and adopted by the grand-parents (Mr. and Mrs. Woodhill) when only twelve days old, and with them she lived until their decease, and for both ever entertained the most loving and devoted affection. Mr. Naden, on the death of his wife, left Francis Street, and also resided at Pakenham House for some considerable time. Twenty-three years afterwards Miss Naden's first volume of poems, *Songs and Sonnets of Springtime*, was dedicated in a sonnet to her grand-parents : and it may be doubted if the English language contains a much more beautiful or tender memorial of filial gratitude.

It was a happy home at Pakenham House. "Little Consie," the pet child-name by which she was

endearingly called in early days, was perfectly idolised
by the grand-parents, who religiously kept every scrap
of her writing and drawing, but they never spoiled
her. Doubtless, as has been pointed out, partly in consequence of living this retired life with elderly people,
she grew up, in the words of her cousin, Miss
Woodhill, "a quaint, retiring, meditative, and silent
child." Nothing remarkable is remembered of her
uneventful childhood, except her extremely retentive
memory and her absolute veracity. A writer in a
local publication truly says :—"So intense was her love
of truth that deception or prevarication were simply
impossible to her." She was baptized in St. Mary's
Church, Birmingham, but while she resided with her
grand-parents she attended—as I am informed by a
relative—the Wycliff, Mount Zion, and Church of the
Redeemer Baptist places of worship. The future
genius was first taught to read by her grandmother,
a lady of refined culture, and of a generous nature—who
many years afterwards endowed a bed at the Jaffray
Convalescent Hospital at a cost of £1,200, the cheque
for which Miss Naden presented to H.R.H. the Prince
of Wales on the occasion of the opening of that valuable
institution in 1885—the method adopted being that of a
little book called "Reading without Tears," where she
learned the words at sight without first learning her
letters. The method commends itself as being in
harmony with that procedure, "from the simple to the
complex," laid down by Mr. Herbert Spencer in his
Education, as illustrated by "the modern course of
placing grammar, not before language, but after it."

Her old nurse and foster-mother (Mrs. Pratt), whom she did not fail to remember in her will, affectionately treasures (and recently exhibited to me with natural pride) a series of seven photographs taken at various periods during the life of her "dear lamented darling," from that of a lovely baby in arms of twelve months until the age of thirty-one years, which show most interestingly the evolution of the features from the earliest commencement up to the highly intellectual face brought out by the well-known Whitlock portrait, taken in 1887, which has been beautifully engraved by Mr. G. J. Stodart, and a copy of which forms the frontispiece to this memoir. The friends and admirers of Miss Naden owe a debt of gratitude to Dr. R. W. Dale, who advised Mr. Whitlock to ask her to sit before her Indian journey, and this life-like photograph was the result. The signature and holograph are facsimiles from the last letter which she wrote to me, October 23rd, 1889.

Miss Maude Michell, of Elvetham Road, Edgbaston, a beloved friend from her earliest years, until the close of life, has been so kind as to supply me with many interesting particulars. She writes:—"In reference to Miss Naden's childhood, may I suggest that her poem, 'Six Years Old,' is almost literally autobiographical. It cannot have been long after this time that the solitary child was joined by a companion, who, though three years younger than herself, distinctly remembers the wall of imaginary antiquity! the lime tree, whose boughs and twigs were converted into bows and arrows ; and the 'talks' with the trees, birds, and butterflies, out of which grew questionings as to 'How?' and 'Why?' these were; what was our relation to them, and theirs to us; questionings to the solution of which the elder of the two devoted her life. In looking back to the last meeting of these friends, on October 26th, 1889, it seems almost prophetic that she dwelt specially upon the beauty of Rossetti's poem, 'Sea Limits,' feeling—but only for the time— as if life was still shrouded in 'The same desire and Mystery' that had baffled the questionings of childhood."

When eight years old she was sent to a small private day school in Frederick Road, Edgbaston, kept by the Misses Martin, two Unitarian ladies of considerable culture, with whom she remained until the age of sixteen or seventeen years, about which period her intellect began to make rapid progress.

Mrs. F. T. S. Houghton, of The Woodlands, Stanmore Road, Edgbaston, another life-long and dear friend, a schoolfellow, and subsequent fellow-student at the Mason College, to whom I am greatly indebted, thus writes to me of these early days:—"The teaching was thorough as far as it went, but entirely lacking in incentives to mental effort. There were no examinations and little competition, so that, although in many subjects Miss Naden enjoyed the distinction of a class to herself, her schoolfellows scarcely realised that there was anything remarkable about the quiet, unassuming girl, who never paraded her talents, and entered with simple enjoyment into all school games and interests. Much time and enthusiasm were given

in the school to flower-painting, and Miss Naden's
first laurels were won in this art, her patient brush
producing the most wonderfully delicate and accurate
studies of flowers from the life—[one of these
studies, a convolvulus, is lovingly preserved by Miss
Dodd, of The Briars, Hagley Road, Edgbaston,
another old friend of early days; and an examination of
the specimen, which was courteously allowed me, and
a second specimen, consisting of a group of pansies,
since kindly presented to me by her cousin, Miss
Woodhill, amply confirm the truth of the above
description]—studies which show little of the freedom
and vigour which characterise her treatment of
intellectual subjects in later life, but which clearly
indicate unusual powers of observation, and an infinite
capacity for taking pains.

"At one time circumstances threw Miss Naden
much into the society of girls younger than herself,
and to them she proved a singularly delightful and
sympathetic companion. She possessed the fascinat-
ing gift of a Princess Scheherazade, or an Andrew
Lang, and used day after day to beguile the tedium
of the walk to school with marvellous fairy tales, in
which fun and fancy, beautiful imaginations, and
grotesque impossibilities were skilfully intermingled,
and the most delicate consideration shown for youthful tastes and prejudices. For example, her good
fairies were invariably lavish of chocolate!"

Miss Maude Michell also writes:—"It is interesting to fill in still further the outline of 'the few years
after leaving school.' At first, general reading and

flower-painting occupied almost her whole time. A picture was accepted by the Birmingham Society of Artists; the following year two, without any apparent cause, were rejected. This was a slight disappointment, but it was the means of directing her thoughts into other channels. French, German, Latin, and Greek were studied in turn, and in 1879, her training in science began."

Among the many books which Miss Naden read in her early years, those relating to Mysticism had a great attraction for her, especially the writings of James Hinton and the Rev. R. A. Vaughan. The "Hours with the Mystics," of the last-mentioned, was always an immense favourite with her, and as its talented author resided in Birmingham for some time, it may not be inappropriate to introduce the following notice of him, which has been kindly contributed by my friend, Mr. E. W. Badger, F.R.H.S., and which has something more than local interest:—"The Rev. Robert Alfred Vaughan, B.A., was a Congregational minister in Birmingham, and resided in Calthorpe Road Edgbaston, a short distance from the Five Ways, on the left hand side going towards Edgbaston Old Church. He was a very noticeable man, and his sermons, which were remarkable in many ways, attracted numbers of the most intellectual people in Birmingham to Ebenezer Chapel, in Steelhouse Lane, during the time he was minister there, viz., from 1850 to 1855. Two years later he died at the early age of thirty-four. He had a handsome and picturesque presence, and in the pulpit often had a seraphic expression of countenance. His sermons were most polished productions, full of thought and refined suggestiveness. They were preached extempore, but every sentence was as polished and as carefully constructed as though it had been laboriously written in his study. These sermons were full of imagery and graphic illustrations drawn from all sorts of sources. There was nothing in the slightest degree extravagant about them, and they had a charm 'of ballad-like simplicity of language' which was utterly unlike anything we are familiar with in most other sermons. 'Hours with the Mystics' was begun and nearly completed during Mr. Vaughan's residence at Birmingham, and was written within a short distance of what was Miss Naden's home for the larger part of her life. 'Hours with the Mystics' was published in two small foolscap 8vo volumes by Messrs. John W. Parker and Son, London, in 1856, and a new edition (the fifth) has recently been issued. It is described on the title page as 'A Contribution to the History of Religious Opinion.' What it aims at doing, and what was actually achieved, may be in some degree gathered from the following extract from the preface:—

'In the religious history of almost every age and country we meet with a certain class of minds, impatient of mere ceremonial forms and technical distinctions, who have pleaded the cause of the heart against prescription, and yielded themselves to the most vehement impulses of the soul, in its longing to escape from the sign to the thing signified—from the human to the divine. The story of such an ambition,

with its disasters and its glories, will not be deemed by
any thoughtful mind less worthy of record than the
career of a conqueror. Through all the changes of
doctrine and the long conflict of creeds, it is interesting
to trace the unconscious unity of mystical tempera-
ments in every communion. It can scarcely be
without some profit that we essay to gather together
and arrange this company of ardent natures ; to account
for their harmony and their differences, to ascertain
the extent of their influence for good and evil, to point
out their errors, and to estimate even dreams impossible
to cold or meaner spirits.' "

In searching for the factors other than those just
alluded to, which gave the bias to her mind in favour
of literature, science, and philosophy, one is certainly
impressed (first) with the important fact, as has been
pointed out to me, that " Miss Naden inherited many
of her mental characteristics from her mother, who
was a woman of no ordinary powers; her keen
sense of humour, often finding vent in witty rhymes,
her impatience of dogmatism, her mind always open
to new modes of thought, and her habit of voracious
reading, all lived again in her child;" (second) with
the ever-present example of her grandfather, Mr.
Woodhill, an intelligent and warm-hearted gentleman,
a great book-lover in his retirement, who possessed
a large miscellaneous library, and of whom the writer
of these lines entertains many pleasant recollections
of "bookish chat" in days gone by. Another friend,
with whom I have conferred, expresses her belief
that Miss Naden "not only read every one of

these books, but that she mastered their contents;"
(third) with the important influence exercised by
her devoted friend and accomplished mentor, Dr.
Robert Lewins, of the Army Medical Department,
who has been justly described as "a man of great
culture, of wide travel, and worldly experience," whom
she first met at Southport in the year 1876. *En
passant*, it is gratifying to record that this loyal friend
has generously founded a gold medal, to be called
"The Constance Naden Medal,"* in her honour at the
Mason College, the subjects of the competitive essay
to vary from year to year, but, when possible, the
preference to be given to philosophical rather than
to special subjects; and he intends to place a
marble bust of her—which is a *chef d'œuvre* of
the sculptor, Mr. William Tyler, of Kensington, by
whom it was exhibited at the Royal Academy this
year—in the library of the College, and to offer a
réplica, or a picture of her, to the National Portrait
Gallery. Dr. Lewins has also edited, and recently
published, at his own cost, a first volume, *Induction
and Deduction* (London: Bickers and Son, 1, Leicester
Square, 1890), a historical and critical sketch of
successive philosophical conceptions respecting the
relations between inductive and deductive thought,

---

* Since these lines were written, it is interesting to record
that the first award of the Constance Naden Gold Medal, founded
by Dr. Lewins, was made by the Council of the Mason College
at their Meeting on Monday, September 30th, 1890, the recipient
being Mr. Frederick Daniel Chattaway, now of Christ Church,
Oxford.   Mr. Chattaway's contribution was a poem entitled
" Persephone—a myth re-set."

and other essays, being a selection from Miss Naden's philosophical writings, to which is prefixed an admirable and sympathetic memoir, written by her friend and companion, Mrs. Daniell. A fourth minor factor of influence may have been the late Mr. William Bates, B.A., sometime classical tutor of Queen's College, Birmingham, a great bibliophile, an indefatigable collector, and author of a memoir of George Cruikshank, and other works, who was her instructor in the classics.

But, in spite of a somewhat restricted environment, the primary germs of love of knowledge were indubitably obtained from the grand-parents, whom she thus recognises in the beautiful dedicatory sonnet previously referred to :—

Ye who received me, when your hearts were sore,
    With double welcome, since I came in lieu
    Of one whose fond embrace I never knew—
Your child, my mother, dear for evermore—
Who scarce had time to greet the babe she bore,
    But, dying in her spring, bequeathed to you,
    Her father and her mother, guardians true,
One little life, to tend when hers was o'er :

Ye who have watched me from my infant days
    With tenderest love and care, who treasure yet
Quaint sayings, sketches rude, and childish lays,
    Accept this wreath, entwined in April hours :
Yours was the garden where the seed was set,
    To you I dedicate the opening flowers.

The uneventful routine of home life was first broken by a little visit to her old friends and former governesses, the Misses Martin, who had removed to Clevedon, and subsequently by an annual trip to the sea-side and other watering-places. In the summer of 1881, in company with her friend, Miss Ellen Brown, she visited Belgium, went up the Rhine, and through Switzerland, returning home by way of Paris. Her fellow-traveller thus writes to me :—" I look back upon the long summer weeks spent in her sweet society as one of the brightest spots in an altogether happy period of my life." In the spring of 1883 she travelled for some months in Italy, in company with Miss Rock, and her letters graphically describe the beauties of the Riviera, Genoa, Rome, Venice, Naples, etc. During this tour I am informed that "she acquired a knowledge of Italian, and very soon after her return was able to translate Dante with ease." But this by the way.

For a time Miss Naden taught at the Home for Friendless Girls, in Bristol Street, Birmingham, an institution in which she took some interest.

And now we are approaching the most important epoch in her career. "For a few years," writes Mrs. Houghton, " after leaving school, Miss Naden led a quiet secluded life, devoting herself to the systematic study of languages, and mastering in turn French, German, Latin, and the elements of Greek. To this period belong the *Songs and Sonnets of Springtime*, most of which were composed at odd moments, for Miss Naden believed with Goethe that 'nothing is so precious as time.'"

Another writer (Miss Evans, a friend and former fellow-student), in an interesting biography in the *Mason College Magazine*, for February, 1890, states that the charming dedicatory sonnet above quoted "was composed while the poetess was occupied with domestic duties to relieve her grandmother!" and Miss Naden told the same friend "that most of her poems were composed while she was dressing in the morning, and most of her thinking done on her way to college."

During the sessions of 1879-80 and 1880-1 Miss Naden attended the Botany Classes and the Field Classes in connection therewith, at the Birmingham and Midland Institute, under Mr. J. W. Oliver, the present lecturer on Botany, and took first-class certificates at the examinations of the Science and Art Department. Mr. Oliver speaks with admiration of his modest and unassuming, but diligent and clever pupil—always punctual, as his attendance book shows—ever working with growing enthusiasm, who answered his questions promptly, and the answers were generally correct. She also attended the German and French classes at the Institute, under the late lamented Dr. Dammann; and Mr. W. H. Cope, the courteous librarian of the Mason College, favours me with the following interesting anecdote, which he heard from the doctor, of her proficiency in the German language. Dr. Dammann was conducting his class at the Institute one evening, when the students were going through one of the German authors, each student taking it in turn to read and translate a passage into English. The passage under consideration contained a lengthy quotation from one of the Greek writers. Upon reaching this, the student translating suddenly came

to a dead stop.   Dr. Dammann thought he would like
to see if anyone in the class could give a translation
of the Greek quotation in *modern German*, although,
as he told my informant, he fancied there was only
one student who would be likely to attempt it—and
that was Miss Naden—so he asked her to give them
a German rendering, feeling that she would be able to
get through it somehow; but he confessed himself
surprised and delighted at the ease and rapidity with
which she attacked the passage, and gave her hearers
a masterly translation of the quotation in modern
German.   Dr. Dammann told Mr. Cope that he
looked upon her as the most brilliant pupil he had
ever had in his professional career.   The Midland
Institute are naturally proud of their distinguished
student, for, in the *Institute Magazine* of March, 1890,
the editor says :—" We are glad to find that we may
regard her rare gifts as in some measure nourished by
our Alma Mater, and herself as one of us."

Her attendance at the Botany Classes came to
an end in 1881, but her thirst for knowledge was
unappeased, as she had already been struck by the
relation of one science to all, and she grew eager to
master them all one by one.   An opportunity of a
rare kind soon presented itself.

In the autumn of 1881 she entered as a student of
the Mason College, to which noble institution she was
indebted for a thoroughly sound scientific training.
Of this "momentous event" Mrs. Houghton thus
writes :—"Not only did it open out to her immeasurably
wider fields of knowledge, but it brought the hitherto

solitary student into the midst of a bright, active little intellectual world, and gave her those companionships and interests which were a positive need of her essentially genial and sociable mind. In this congenial atmosphere Miss Naden developed like a plant brought out of semi-darkness into sunshine—not so strikingly, perhaps, in intellect as in character. It was at Mason College, in the lively debates of the Union, the pleasant but not always peaceful discussions of the Poesy Club, and the learned disquisitions of the various scientific societies, that Miss Naden first became conscious of the full extent of her powers, and assumed that leadership which was her birthright. When she rose to speak there was always a thrill of expectation ; her audience knew that however 'thrashed out' by previous speakers the subject might be, it would exhibit fresh vitality and present a new aspect under her skilful treatment; and the hearts of her opponents sank as they thought of the weak points and hidden sophistries in their arguments. Miss Naden had a terrible sixth sense for such things, and dealt with them with a satire which was playful or severe as occasion demanded. Needless to say that this gift did not tend to make her popular with those in whom *amour propre* was more largely developed than the sense of humour. But if Miss Naden was swift to detect error and absurdity (and perhaps the Union debates afforded exceptional scope for destructive criticism), she was equally prompt to recognise a good point or a fine thought, and gave unstinted honour where honour was due."

It will be fitting in this place to enter a little into detail in explaining another factor—a new environment —which, coming just as it did towards the end of her college career, had a profound influence in the future on Miss Naden's conceptions of the science of life, and its correlative, the science of society. During the spring of the year 1883 an important departure from its ordinary work was resolved upon by the Birmingham Natural History and Microscopical Society — the oldest existing scientific society in the town. On the requisition of fifteen members, the Council unanimously resolved to establish a Sociological Section for the study of Mr. Herbert Spencer's system of " Synthetic Philosophy." The Society already had Geological, Biological, and Microscopical Sections, and this last addition was naturally the complement of its operations. The project was inaugurated with the hearty approval of Mr. Spencer himself, who addressed a valuable letter to the President on the occasion; the first hon. sec. being Mr. Alfred Hayes, M.A., the present accomplished Secretary of the Birmingham and Midland Institute, and author of that exquisite poem, *The Last Crusade*, and other works. Since the establishment of the Section, nearly the whole of the works of " our great philosopher " have been considered and subjected to an exhaustive and searching exposition and criticism, in which most of those students in the town and neighbourhood actively interested in the spread of the doctrine of evolution have at times taken part ; the proceedings whereof have been published from time to time in the *Midland Naturalist*, the organ of the parent Society. To this Section, over which the writer of these lines has had the honour of presiding since its formation, Miss Naden was attracted in the year 1884, and she continued to be a regular member of it until she left Birmingham. Of the many diligent and enthusiastic students of the doctrine of evolution who have assisted at our meetings in discussions, and by readings, criticisms, and expositions, from learned professors and local scientists down to tyros who were just beginning to understand and appreciate Herbert Spencer, not one was so highly valued as Miss Naden.

It may be interesting to place on record the names of some of the members and friends who have chiefly rendered assistance to the Section by reading papers, and in other ways, most of whom were Miss Naden's colleagues :—Professor F. J. Allen, M.A., Mr. C. H. Allison, Mr. J. O. W. Barratt, B.Sc., Mr. Alfred Browett, Mrs. Alfred Browett, Mr. Harold W. Buncher, Miss Byett, Mr. F. J. Cullis, F.G.S., Miss Dalton, Miss Jane Kerr Davies, Mr. W. Greatheed, Mr. W. B. Grove, M.A., Miss Goyne, Professor Haycraft, M.A., F.R.S. Ed., Dr. Hiepe, Dr. Alfred Hill, F.I.C., Mr. Edwin Hill, Mr. J. Alfred Hill, F.R.M.S., Professor Hillhouse, M.A., F.L.S., Mr. L. J. Major, Mr. William Mathews, M.A., F.G.S., Mr. W. Kineton Parkes, Professor Poynting, D.Sc., F.R.S., Mr. Herbert Stone, F.L.S., and Mr. Colbran J. Wainwright.

At these meetings, held in the Society's room at the Mason College, she was an immense favourite—the *genius loci* in fact—and from the wide range of her knowledge, the lucidity and force of her intellect, and the richness of her illustrations, she never failed when speaking to impress her audience and carry complete conviction. But, although a scientist and a philosopher as well, her womanly grace and her womanly sympathy were always dominant. Even on removal to a distant home, her interest in the Section and her friendships with her old colleagues did not cease, for she specially came down from London twice to take a prominent part in its proceedings, and, as one of the speakers happily remarked at a subsequent meeting, "helped it in crises of its history."

Thoroughly equipped as she had been at the Mason College with a sound knowledge of the sciences—physics, chemistry, botany, zoology, physiology, and geology—with refined literary, artistic, and poetical tastes that were pursued as mere diversion, and following the example of the Master by not striving for the honours of a college degree, her broad sympathies lay beyond the somewhat exclusive work in the domain of the specialist, and thus the first determination of her bias for the philosophy of evolution, as embraced in the "Synthetic Philosophy," was doubtless manifested in her address on *Special Creation and Evolution*, delivered before a meeting of the Section, held January 22nd, 1885, in which year she was subsequently awarded the "Panton Prize" at the Mason College, for the best essay on "the Geology of the District." Her second address on *The Data of Ethics* was given before the Section, February 22nd, 1887.

In the same year, and while still a student of the College, she wrote her brilliant essay, *Induction and Deduction*, which gained the "Heslop Gold Medal," founded and endowed by the late Dr. Heslop, and which is the highest prize that has ever been offered to the past and present students of the Mason College.

A few words may be interesting respecting the nature of this prize. It is awarded annually by the Council for the best dissertation or essay upon a subject which the candidate has the privilege of selecting. The Academic Board of the College issues annually, before the 25th December, a list of subjects in divisions, thus classified :—(*a*) Language, Literature, and Philosophy; (*b*) Mathematical and Physical Sciences, including Metallurgy and Engineering; (*c*) Biological and Geological Science, including Mining. One of these divisions only is selected for each year, and in 1887, the philosophical division was chosen, and Miss Naden's thesis obtained the prize.

It was a natural sequence from analysis to synthesis, and these contributions and others were the rich fruits of that determination. In further illustration of this mental attitude, it is pleasant to relate, on the authority of her friend, Dr. Lewins, an incident of her Eastern tour. She told Lord Dufferin, in India, when he complimented her on her poems, that she meant her real mission to be philosophy, "not harsh and crabbed as dull fools suppose, but musical as is Apollo's lute," to which the Governor General replied, "Ah! I am no judge of that."

Ever since her connection with the Section, she brought to bear on her criticism the canons of the "Synthetic Philosophy," which are simply that the laws of evolution affecting inorganic phenomena are common also to organic and super-organic phenomena, and from this standpoint she rightly viewed society as an organism—a vast organism—as regards its genesis and many-phased development.

An appreciative and valuable memoir of her in *Edgbastonia* for February, 1890, by her friend and former teacher, Professor Lapworth, LL.D., F.R.S., Professor of Geology at the Mason College, confirms this view, and justly says:—"Looking back over her college work as a whole, it appears tolerably clear that her choice of scientific subjects was involuntarily dictated by the special bent of her mind. For from the scientific point of view she was distinctly an evolutionist. She had a mind dominated with an idea of the essential unity of nature, and of man's intimate relationship to all the members of the animate and inanimate worlds. To natural science (and by this term we would include all the sciences she personally studied) she looked for our actual knowledge of man's relationship to nature in general, that she might have firm ground upon which to stand when she worked at her own favourite subject—the relationship of men to each other. This training, acting upon a well-balanced mind, gave her conversation a striking air of originality and freedom of thought. She had a habit of referring everything to first principles, and of utterly ignoring the views of the authoritative specialists. Intensely sympathetic as was her mind for what was novel, wonderful, or strange, it was impatient of everything that was dogmatic or authoritative. The chief enquiry was always not 'What do the specialists say?' but, 'Is it true, and why?' "

Her own practical estimate of her philosophy is thus aptly described in a letter to a friend, quoted in the *Mason College Magazine*, previously referred to:—"My 'philosophy' is to get all the good out of life that it will give, under all circumstances, which involves making the best of trouble, and bearing it so as to gain moral strength; and even if we can't always live up to this ideal, it is good to keep it in sight."

Also, in another letter addressed to Miss Michell, she further emphasises this estimate:—"I do quite agree with you about bodily and mental suffering. It does, in many cases, give us added insight into our own nature, and therefore into human nature in general, with wider and deeper sympathies. It often, too, helps us to cling more closely to our highest ideal, as the only certain refuge from pain and sorrow, and so gives added strength, not only for endurance, but for action. . . . The greatest possible consolation in any sort of suffering is that its effect on you, and therefore upon others, depends largely on yourself; that is the chief moral I have got from life, and it has been a helpful one to me."

And again, in another letter to the same friend:— " So soon as I can feel that I have done anything worth doing, I shall be as happy as anyone can reasonably hope to be. Even if that time never comes, there is much in my life to soften and render bearable the sense of failure."

Further, in a letter written from Calcutta, on February 5th, 1888, to the same friend, she says:— "I know so well that feeling of which you speak—the longing to get rid of all the fetters of self, and to merge one's being in the universe. . . . The true escape from selfishness is reached by self-expansion. I mean that we can never serve humanity in the best way. or completely realise its unity, and our unity with it, unless we have cultivated our own nature to the full, with all its varied powers and sympathies. Only this must be done not for any petty personal ambition, but with a great object in view. I can't cast aside personal ambition and passions, perhaps never shall, till they are either fulfilled, or finally disappointed, but I *do* try not to let them dominate me. . . What you say, while it humiliates me, yet encourages and strengthens me to try to live a braver life, nearer to my ideal of what is good and true."

In all, Miss Naden delivered a series of three addresses or lectures on the doctrine of evolution before the Sociological Section, namely, *Special Creation and Evolution*, *The Data of Ethics* (previously mentioned), and *The Principles of Sociology* (the last of which, recently published in the *Midland Naturalist*, has mournful memories connected with it, and will be presently referred to), which constitute, in an essential form, much of the pith and marrow of the five great divisions of the "Synthetic Philosophy," as originally grouped by Mr. Spencer, in his Prospectus of June 5th, 1862, and to which he has systematically adhered ever since. As a matter of fact these addresses were not delivered in consecutive order. That on *The Data of Ethics* should, of course, have come last; but this is of little moment. Combined, they form a miniature synthetic trilogy, which presents many of the main features of the evolution philosophy, and they may be read with equal profit and advantage either by the tyro or by the advanced student. Speaking generally, they express throughout the highest truth developed by Mr. Spencer's system, that "evolution can end only in the establishment of the greatest perfection and the most complete happiness." The attention of Mr. Spencer was directed to these papers, in which he took much interest, and frequently expressed his approval of them. They were reprinted by the Section, and well circulated among students of the doctrine of evolution in England and America.

To those who accept the Hypothesis of Evolution it will not be necessary to refer in detail for arguments in favour of Miss Naden's thesis on *Special Creation and Evolution*, but it may be interesting to quote a few lines from that on *The Data of Ethics*. After minutely defining the relative claims of egoism and altruism, she thus concludes :—

" But if egoism is essential, and altruism also essential, and yet the two conflict ; what is our hope ? Will the weary battle go on for ever ? Is there no prospect of a final peace ?

"There is such a prospect. We have already seen that evolution works towards perfect adaptation to the environment. Pleasures and pains are not fixed and absolute; they are relative to structures, and to the states of structures; and as organisms adjust themselves physically to the conditions of their life, they must at the same time adjust themselves psychically. That is, every mode of action demanded by social conditions must eventually become pleasurable to social beings, and as parental love is already an instinct, so the broader love, not only of country, but of the race, will in time become instinctive. Sympathy, hitherto stunted by adverse conditions, will develop; and as human nature improves, the natural language of feeling will be less restrained; looks, words, tones will all grow more expressive, and the power of interpreting them will strengthen and sharpen by use. As the sphere of sympathetic gratification widens, the sphere of self-sacrifice will diminish; for with growing efficiency and increasing welfare there will be fewer troubles to assuage, fewer pangs to partake. No one will be willing to accept benefits at the cost of pain or privation to others. . . . It is this conception of the completely adapted man in the completely evolved society with which moral science must deal, just as physics and astronomy must assume in the first place certain ideal conditions, making allowance subsequently for actual incidental conditions. The rigid and weightless lever is a fiction; the ideal man is a fiction; but both are fictions which have a direct and practical bearing on reality. Only, while the physicist's lever can never become a reality, the moralist's man may yet tread the earth in flesh and blood ; ethically adult, having outgrown that sense of self-control and self-compulsion, which is so often painful to the best of us ; no more conscious of the demands of duty than he is conscious of the beatings of his own heart. Here philosophy and poetry meet and clasp hands; for the picture drawn by Mr. Spencer cannot be distinguished from that drawn by Wordsworth in his ' Ode to Duty : '

> ' Serene will be our days and bright,
>   And happy will our nature be
> When love is an unerring light,
>   And joy its own security.
> And they a blissful course may hold,
> Even now, who not unwisely bold,
> Live in the spirit of this creed,
> Yet find that other strength, according to their need.' "

Miss Naden was a prolific prose writer in other departments, and as she sometimes wrote under her full name, and oftener by modestly abbreviated initials (C.N. only), and sometimes under the *nom de plume* of "Constance Arden," or the initials (C.A.), it is not an easy matter to compile a bibliography, but among philosophical and other contributions, the following may be specially mentioned, viz. :—In the *Journal of Science* :—" Hylozoism v. Animism," 1881 (C.N.) ; "The Identity of Vital and Cosmical Energy" (C. N.); " Animal Automatism " (Constance Arden) ; and " The Philosophy of Thomas Carlyle" (Constance Arden), 1882 ; "The Brain Theory of Mind and Matter " (Constance Arden) ; and " Paracelsus "

(Constance C. W. Naden), 1883; "Hylo-idealism" (C. A.); and "Hylo-idealism: a Defence" (C. N.), 1884. In *Knowledge* :—"The Sentient World" (C.N.); "Hylo-idealism: Does a Universe Exist Exterior to Ourselves?" (C. N.); "The Evolution of the Sense of Beauty" (Constance C. W. Naden); "Conceptions and Images" (C. N.); "Idealism" (C. N.); "The Weak Point of Darwinism" (Constance C. W. Naden), 1885. In the *Agnostic Annual* :—"Pessimism and Physiology," 1885; and "Are Miracles Credible?" 1890. In *London Society* :—"The Lady Doctor," 1877. So far back as 1883 she published, under initials (C. N.), a pamphlet, "What is Religion?" a vindication of freethought; and in 1887, also under initials (C. N.), a preface to a series of letters in a pamphlet by her friend Dr. Lewins, entitled "Hylo-idealism, the Creed of the Coming Day." Writing to a friend subsequently on the subject of orthodox belief, she says :—"The religion of the future will be a more vivid feeling of life—not of one's own life, but of life in general—a sort of extended sympathy. So that we shall shrink from doing anything that is against the general laws of happiness, even when it seems to make for our own happiness. At least, that is the ideal which seems to me the true one." An elaborate paper by her, on "Volition," was read at the meeting of the Mason College Physiological Society, February 8th, 1887, and appears in Vol. XI. of the *Midland Naturalist*, 1888. Referring to this paper, she wrote to a friend :—"It is very dry, I believe. Several people spoke afterwards to the effect that they had

profited extremely, but hadn't understood a word."
In the *Scottish Art Review*, for April, 1889, there
appeared an interesting review by her of Mr. Robert
Buchanan's epic poem, "The City of Dream." Space
only permits the bare mention of these numerous articles
to indicate the depth, the boldness, and the versatility
of her talent. Her contributions to the *Mason College
Magazine*, which she edited for a time, are referred to
elsewhere.

It may be mentioned, for the encouragement of
future authors, that the first prose essay which Miss
Naden sent to a publisher was rejected; and that an
eminent firm of publishers in London declined
her second volume of poems—although she offered
to defray the whole cost of publication, as is usual
with most young poets—fearing it would discredit
their establishment!

Miss Naden was a member of the Ladies' Debating Society in Birmingham, and succeeded Mrs. R. W.
Dale and Mrs. Crosskey as president. Her address
for the session 1882-3—a most finished performance—
is founded on a belief that "the watchword of the
coming day is Unity, built up from Diversity," and
thus concludes :—"Every utterance of a true and
lofty idea, in word or deed, helps to render possible
a new heroic age—an age which shall find its chief
glory, not in commerce or manufactures, not in
discoveries and inventions, but in a life moulded to
that higher expediency, which we call Truth and
Justice, instead of the lower expediency, which may
take the shape of Justice or Injustice, Truth or False-
hood."

Miss Naden published two volumes of poems.
The first of these *Songs and Sonnets of Springtime*,
1881, of which mention has already been made,
contains beautiful specimens of the "opening flowers"
which subsequently developed into rich fruit. Next
to the "Dedication," which has been previously
referred to, the masterpiece is undoubtedly "The
Pantheist's Song of Immortality," described by Mr.
Gladstone as "a short but singularly powerful production." It is so beautiful that her admirers will,
I am sure, be pleased to read it in this place :—

THE PANTHEIST'S SONG OF IMMORTALITY.

Bring snow-white lilies, pallid heat-flushed roses,
   Enwreathe her brow with heavy-scented flowers ;
In soft undreaming sleep her head reposes,
   While, unregretted, pass the sunlit hours.

Few sorrows did she know—and all are over ;
   A thousand joys—but they are all forgot :
Her life was one fair dream of friend and lover ;
   And were they false—ah, well, she knows it not.

Look in her face, and lose thy dread of dying ;
   Weep not, that rest will come, that toil will cease:
Is it not well, to lie as she is lying,
   In utter silence, and in perfect peace ?

Canst thou repine, that sentient days are numbered?
   Death is unconscious Life, that waits for birth :
So didst thou live, while yet thine embryo slumbered,
   Senseless, unbreathing, e'en as heaven and earth.

Then shrink no more from Death, though Life be
    gladness,
  Nor seek him, restless in thy lonely pain :
The law of joy ordains each hour of sadness,
  And firm or frail, thou canst not live in vain.

What though thy name by no sad lips be spoken,
  And no fond heart shall keep thy memory green?
Thou yet shalt leave thine own enduring token,
  For earth is not as though thou ne'er hadst been.

See yon broad current, hasting to the ocean,
  Its ripples glorious in the western red :
Each wavelet passes, trackless ; yet its motion
  Has changed for evermore the river bed.

Ah, wherefore weep, although the form and fashion
  Of what thou seemest, fades like sunset flame ?
The uncreated Source of toil and passion,
  Through everlasting change abides the same.

Yes, thou shalt die : but these almighty forces,
  That meet to form thee, live for evermore :
They hold the suns in their eternal courses,
  And shape the tiny sand-grains on the shore.

Be calmly glad, thine own true kindred seeing
  In fire and storm, in flowers with dew impearled ;
Rejoice in thine imperishable being,
  One with the Essence of the boundless world."

I am indebted to my friend, Mr. E. C. Copas,
M.A., of the Handsworth Bridge Trust Grammar

School, for pointing out to me what in my judgment appears to be highly significant of the growing appreciation of Miss Naden's writings in high quarters. At the Examination at Oxford, for the Jesus College Scholarships and Exhibitions, April, 1890, the first three verses of this poem were selected by the authorities as the passage set for Latin Elegiacs.

The charming little poem, "Six Years Old," indicates her early and remarkable powers of observation, and as already has been pointed out, is mostly autobiographical. Her second volume, *A Modern Apostle, The Elixir of Life, The Story of Clarice, and other Poems*, 1887, unmistakably shows an advance on her earlier publication, influenced, no doubt, by her studies in evolution, and especially in physiology and psychology. As regards the "Evolutional Erotics"—one of the divisions of the book—we must go to Dr. Wendell Holmes if we want similar expositions of the marvellous blending of science with poetry as those gems which Miss Naden here presents. One of them "Solomon Redivivus, 1886," which illustrates the development of life "from Darwin and from Buddh," astonished us by the remarkable spontaneity of her genius. At one of our sectional meetings the subject had been discussed in the evening, and the next morning the President received a copy of the poem by post. As a contrast in style to the "Pantheist's Song," and as showing Miss Naden's capability to handle some of the most recondite speculations of modern

philosophy in a sprightly and satirical, yet thoughtful,
vein, I cannot resist the temptation to present this
poem in full :—

SOLOMON REDIVIVUS, 1886.

What am I?   Ah, you know it,
　　I am the modern Sage,
Seer, savant, merchant, poet—
　　I am, in brief, the Age.

Look not upon my glory
　　Of gold and sandal-wood,
But sit and hear a story
　　From Darwin and from Buddh.

Count not my Indian treasures,
　　All wrought in curious shapes,
My labours and my pleasures,
　　My peacocks and my apes ;

For when you ask me riddles,
　　And when I answer each,
Until my fifes and fiddles
　　Burst in and drown our speech,

Oh then your soul astonished
　　Must surely faint and fail,
Unless, by me admonished,
　　You hear our wondrous tale.

D

We were a soft Amœba
  In ages past and gone,
Ere you were Queen of Sheba,
  And I King Solomon.

Unorganed, undivided,
  We lived in happy sloth,
And all that you did I did,
  One dinner nourished both :

Till you incurred the odium
  Of fission and divorce—
A severed pseudopodium
  You strayed your lonely course.

When next we met together
  Our cycles to fulfil,
Each was a bag of leather,
  With stomach and with gill.

But our Ascidian morals
  Recalled that old mischance,
And we avoided quarrels
  By separate maintenance.

Long ages passed—our wishes
  Were fetterless and free,
For we were jolly fishes,
  A-swimming in the sea.

We roamed by groves of coral,
  We watched the youngsters play—
The memory and the moral
  Had vanished quite away.

Next, each became a reptile,
　With fangs to sting and slay ;
No wiser ever crept, I'll
　Assert, deny who may.

But now, disdaining trammels
　Of scale and limbless coil,
Through every grade of mammals
　We passed with upward toil.

Till, anthropoid and wary
　Appeared the parent ape,
And soon we grew less hairy
　And soon began to drape.

So, from that soft Amœba,
　In ages past and gone,
You've grown the Queen of Sheba,
　And I, King Solomon.

Those friends who were present at a social gathering of the Section, held in the autumn of the year 1885 at Handsworth Wood, will not easily forget the bright and playful humour with which she recited "Scientific Wooing," another poem in the same series. On its publication, the author of this memoir sent a short critical notice of this beautiful volume to the *Midland Naturalist* for July, 1887, and he treasures among other letters and relics of his beloved friend the following appreciative acknowledgment, which it is most interesting to record as showing her feelings generally towards her Birmingham friends :—

Pakenham House, Edgbaston, June 29th, 1887.

Dear Mr. Hughes,

Thank you very much for your kind review of my book. It is much more than kind, because it emphasises those aspects of my writing which I have more especially at heart.

Thank you also for your sympathy. I can scarcely as yet realise all that this loss means to me. I shall travel for some time, and finally settle in London ; but I do not mean to let this change of abode sever any of my old friendships and interests. I shall always feel grateful to the Sociological Section and to its President.

With very kind regards to Mrs. Hughes and to yourself,

Believe me, yours sincerely,

CONSTANCE C. W. NADEN.

The loss above alluded to was the death of her grandmother, Mrs. J. C. Woodhill, June 21st, 1887, which happened on Her Majesty's Jubilee, and while all England was rejoicing, Miss Naden was plunged in deep sorrow in her lonely home. Her grandfather died December 27th, 1881.

Her first volume contains an original poem in German of great beauty and power, " Das Ideal," expressive of her hylo-ideal *rationale* of existence, and both volumes have a few translations from the German and Italian, the most noteworthy of which are " The Knight of Toggenburg," from Schiller, in her first volume, and "Ideals," from the same author, and the "Fragments from Faust," in her second volume. The pretty cloth cover to these volumes was from a design of her own, founded on that rare and exquisite little plant, the ivy-leaved bell-flower, *Campanula hederacea.* On its publication, she sent copies of her second volume to several poets, and I recollect her

showing me with great satisfaction the kindly acknow-
ledgments which she received from the late Matthew
Arnold and Mr. Andrew Lang.

The *Birmingham Weekly Mercury* for January
25th, 1890, printed some unpublished verses of Miss
Naden's, entitled "Night" and "Morning," from a
MS. collection entitled "Songs of the Heart and
Mind," written eleven years ago, when the authoress
was scarcely twenty-one. The *Open Court* (Chicago)
for March 27th and April 3rd, 1890, also published
two posthumous sonnets by Miss Naden—(1) "Un-
discerned Perfection," and (2) "The Pessimist's
Vision."

In a survey of the "British Poetry of the Nine-
teenth Century," published in the second number of
The Speaker for January 11, 1890, that accomplished
critic, the Right Hon. W. E. Gladstone, M.P., places
the name of Miss Naden in a list of eight leading
poetesses having claims to high distinction, Mrs.
Barrett Browning being placed first, while he denies
the title of "Poet" to George Eliot, to Mrs. Hemans,
Joanna Baillie, and indeed all prior to Mrs. Browning,
and thus concludes a very comprehensive article :—
"Upon the whole it may perhaps be allowable to say
not only that the British poetesses of the last sixty
years have developed in numerous instances splendid
powers, but even that they are as a whole without a
parallel in literary history." It is a very high estimate
coming from such a competent authority, but from
subsequent evidence it is probable from the letter
which he addressed to her friend, Mrs. Daniell, who

afterwards sent him a copy of *The Modern Apostle*, that
Mr. Gladstone had not had under his notice Miss
Naden's second volume, which, as before stated, is a
marked advance on her first publication.   She ceased
to write poems in 1887, but, after all, poetry was mere
amusement to her, for she had, as we know, deeper
and more exalted work for her intellectual powers.

II.

"O life as futile, then, as frail !
    O for thy voice to soothe and bless !
    What hope of answer, or redress ?
    Behind the veil, behind the veil."

In Memoriam, TENNYSON.

After leaving Birmingham, on the death of her grandmother, from whom she inherited a very handsome fortune, Miss Naden started, September 29th, 1887, with her friend, Mrs. Daniell, for an extended tour, proceeding across Germany and down the Danube, stopping at Vienna, Buda-Pesth, and other interesting places, on their way to Constantinople—the approach thereto by the Bosphorus, in the early morning, being described as "one of the sensations which are not often repeated in this life"—where a pause was made ; then on to Broussa, Cyprus, Smyrna, Baalbec, Damascus, Palestine, and Cairo. After a trip up the Nile to Assouan, they returned to Cairo, and from thence proceeded to Bombay and Calcutta, their furthest stage being Darjeeling, close to the highest Himalaya range, and they subsequently made the tour of the principal towns of the north-west Provinces, including Agra, Delhi, Benares, Lucknow, Cawnpore, Jeypur, &c. In her interesting memoir, previously referred to, Mrs. Daniell has given a graphic picture of this delightful tour, and she specially mentions, among other reminiscences, that "Miss Naden thoroughly enjoyed and appreciated that never-to-be-forgotten three weeks voyage to Assouan and back, commencing with the Pyramids of Gheezeh, ascending that of Cheops and penetrating into its central sepulchral chamber. Of all the marvels on the Nile, including Thebes, Luxor, Phylae, &c., the great temple and avenues of the Sphinxes, at Karnak, as seen by moonlight, seemed to impress her most. Their grandeur, solemnity, and associations, actually made her kneel, from an over-mastering impulse of reverential awe."

The ladies were received with courtesy and hospitality, both by Lord Dufferin, the Governor General, and by Lord and Lady Reay. In a letter to a friend, Miss Naden says :—"We had a few introductions in Bombay, and I was decidedly amused to find myself plunged into 'the best society,' and meeting the Duchess of Connaught quite informally at a dinner party. She asked me about Mason College, and I had to explain to her the mode of conducting an impromptu debate. Then we were passed on to the Viceroy in Calcutta, and he liked my poems very much, and amused me by saying that he himself 'couldn't write verse, but could do poetical prose very well.'" Professor Max Müller had kindly given them introductions to several of the native pundits, notably to Mr. Malabari, the great Indian reformer of Bombay, now in England, who explained his ideas on the necessary social reforms, especially regarding infant marriages, and the marriage of child-widows. These were alluded to in her subsequent address to the Sociological Section, and in the same paper she records with gratification the fact "that Mr. Spencer's works are known and appreciated among the more highly educated of the native gentlemen." In another letter to a friend, she says :—" We went up to a stupid place, called Mount Aboo, for two days, and the Indian-demon, fever, kept me a prisoner there for seven weeks." Poor lady! it was the last long holiday she ever took, and, although it must have been eminently rich in experiences, reading between the lines, one sees the beginning of the end. The friends returned to London in June, 1888.

On settling down in town after her Indian tour, she resided in apartments, first at 14, Half Moon Street, afterwards at 19, Old Quebec Street, for a time ; and subsequently purchased, in October, 1888, an elegant newly-built house, No. 114, Park Street, Grosvenor Square, in the furnishing and fitting-up of which she took much interest, and her affectionate disposition and intellectual power soon attracted an appreciative circle of cultured and like-minded friends. Of these days, so full of brightness and hope, she thus writes to a friend :—"I am writing, and buying furniture, and going to lectures, and indulging sometimes in mild dissipation, and learning the value of money—I mean how far it *won't* go—which I never had the slightest idea of before. It is all very interesting." She scarcely does herself justice in this latter respect, for I am credibly informed that she had the command of other private means in the lifetime of her grand-parents, out of which the cost of her publications was defrayed, as well as her expenses of travel.

Philosophy still had the greatest fascination for her; she became a member of the Aristotelian Society, and was much valued by her fellow-members, and took an active part in its meetings; indeed, two papers of hers, "On Rationalist and Empiricist Ethics" and "On Mental Physiology and its Place in Philosophy," were announced in the list of papers for January 20th, 1890, and were, since her decease, vicariously read at this Society during the present year. That she was in her element in this learned Society, and could hold her own, is evidenced by an extract from a letter addressed to me, December 22nd, 1888 :—" I had a little discussion with —— [naming a distinguished evolutionist] the other day at the Aristotelian Society, to which I belong, and made him confess that he didn't know his ' Data of Ethics.' The point was, whether Herbert Spencer acknowledges 'the influence of the religious, as well as of the political and social controls, in the evolution of the moral control.'" Professor Dunstan has since published in the " Proceedings of the Aristotelian Society," 1889-90, a brief but very appreciative memoir of his friend and colleague; which, in concluding, states that "by her death the Society loses one of its most valuable members." She was also a member of the Royal Institution, and in the season 1888-9 attended most of its Friday evening lectures, her scientific training enabling her to thoroughly appreciate the subjects introduced.

In the *Pall Mall Gazette* of 7th March, 1889, there appeared an editorial note with some complimentary references to our Sociological Section in Birmingham, and suggesting the formation of a Spencer Society in London. This was promptly followed next day by a letter from Sir Philip Magnus, which it is interesting to record :—

A SPENCER SOCIETY.

To the Editor of the *Pall Mall Gazette.*

Sir,—Your suggestion about a "Spencer Society" is too valuable to remain unnoticed. As a very humble student of philosophy and science, I know how much these two great branches of learning owe, in their mutual relation and dependence, to the great thinker of the present century; but to Herbert Spencer more than to any other writer are undoubtedly due the recent advance of practical education and such improvements as have been introduced into our methods of instruction. His influence is now being felt in all our boys' and girls' schools. His advocacy of science-teaching has partially succeeded in revolutionizing our system of education from the elementary school to the University. What remains to be done can best be done by giving effect to the views expressed in his four articles, which appeared in the *Westminster Review* in the years 1854-9. If our scientists, philosophers, and educationists unite, a Spencer Society may be formed, which may do honour to the author of " First Principles," and may perpetuate his influence. I believe there are many who, like myself, would be glad to assist in the formation of such a Society.

Yours obediently,
PHILIP MAGNUS.

Athenæum, March 7th, 1889.

Miss Naden took immense interest in the proposition, and, with the hearty co-operation of Sir Philip Magnus, exerted herself among her friends in order to establish a Spencer, or Evolution Society in London. I had the pleasure of meeting Sir Philip Magnus at her house at Easter following, and had many chats and some correspondence with her on the subject. She expressed her intention to act as Honorary Secretary to the proposed Society, and suggested that the preliminary meetings might be held in her drawing room; but for her untimely death there is no doubt that she would have, with her usual energy and devotion to the cause of evolution, succeeded in carrying into effect the object suggested. The following letter, which I received some weeks afterwards, explains to what extent she had progressed in the development of her plans:—

114, Park Street,
Grosvenor Square, W.,
May 25th, 1889.

Dear Mr. Hughes,—I have delayed writing to you till I had some progress to report, and now I have not much. But first I must thank you for the *Birmingham Faces and Places*, with its excellent portrait and biography of yourself. I was very much interested in the sketch of your life, which does, as you say, help to account for your "Synthetic sympathies."

Sir Philip Magnus called on me yesterday, in response to another letter which I had written, and we had a talk about the plan —not altogether an encouraging talk, but still I think something may be arranged, though not exactly in the form which we originally contemplated. Sir Philip's experience is precisely the same as mine— that people are strongly disinclined to join a society which calls itself by the name of any one philosopher, however eminent as a scientific thinker. It seems both to him and to me that this feeling is too strong to permit the formation of a "Spencer Society," which would have any real vitality. But it occurred to me that by a change of name we might overcome the difficulty—that we might adopt the title, say, of the "Evolution Society," and, while bringing Mr. Spencer's works prominently forward, might thus be able to invite the co-operation of Evolutionists of different shades of thought. Sir Philip also thinks this a practicable idea. I think I can secure the support of Mr. Clodd—who unfortunately is just now weak and ill after a bad attack of congestion of the lungs— and Professor Rhys Davids, who, of course, is a great authority on the evolution of religions. He was dining with us [*i.e.*, Mrs. Daniell and herself] a few days ago, and I spoke to him on the subject. To-morrow we are dining with some clever people —Dr. and Mrs. Philpot, who, I think, would also be acquisitions. He is the author of the *New Judgment of Paris*, but I fancy he is more than a mere novelist, (I use the word "mere" only as regards our present purposes).

I hope soon to have further progress to report. I thought a preliminary meeting might be held here about the middle of June, but Sir Philip considers that too early, and suggests the second week in July. However, I hope we shall at last get the idea into something like practical shape.

With very kind regards to Mrs. Hughes and to yourself,

Believe me,
Yours very sincerely,
CONSTANCE C. W. NADEN.

In the summer of 1889, writing to me in a letter, dated 4th August, from Ilkley Wells, where she had gone for a little rest, she mentioned, with evident gratification, that she had, at the request of Mr. Herbert Spencer, written "a reply to Mr. Lilly's libel on Utilitarianism in the *Fortnightly*," but, from what she said in a subsequent letter, Mr. Spencer thought it too long for publication in a magazine, but considered the "main point good when reached." It is satisfactory to announce, that this paper will hereafter be published by Dr. Lewins, in a second volume of Miss Naden's posthumous writings. In explanation of its non-appearance in the *Fortnightly*, Dr. Lewins, in a letter to me, says "that she was abreast, and indeed ahead, to some extent, of the epoch, and all successful reviews must be rather behind it to cater for the vast majority of readers who are in a like predicament." Her main energies, however, were devoted to an important work on "Evolutionary Ethics" (included in Dr. Lewins' first volume, previously mentioned), the nucleus of which was the paper read before the Sociological Section on the "Data of Ethics," already referred to, and on the 20th July, in the same year, she thus wrote to me, in reply to a letter :—" My book gets on slowly, but I hope surely. I cannot say when it will be finished, though it won't be a ' mag. op. ' at all, for ideas have an uncomfortable habit of developing as one writes, and of requiring alterations in their clothing."

Many complimentary editorial notices have appeared respecting this volume (*Induction and Deduction*) in the magazines and newspapers during the current year, but none more just and appreciative than that contained in an article entitled " Philosophy and Theology" in the *Westminster Review* for November, 1890, which says :—" There is a pathetic interest attaching to Miss Naden's Essays, as the gifted writer is already beyond the reach of criticism, having died last December, in only her thirty-second year. The readers of these papers will not hesitate to endorse the unstinted praise her friends lavish on her powers, as they are the most unquestionable evidence of an exceptionally gifted and cultivated mind."

In a "Summary of Results" of the first and most important essay in her volume, which does not attempt to give a sketch of the history of philosophy in general, but only such portions of it as bear upon her subject, ranging from the Greek Cosmologists to the great thinkers of our own day, Miss Naden says :—"Briefly all induction which passes (in common phrase) from the 'known to the unknown,' does so by 'parity of reasoning.'

"The new formula for the mutual relations of induction and deduction must run as follows :—Induction is a process of cognition involving recognitions. Deduction is a process of recognition involving cognitions."

As supplementary to the three "primary controls" of Mr. Herbert Spencer in the evolution of morality, viz., the "religious control," the "political control," and the "social control," Miss Naden ventures, in "Evolutionary Ethics," the second essay in her volume, to add a fourth—the *Natural control.*

"I mean [she says] that self-guidance which follows from a more or less definite knowledge of natural processes and consequently of the natural or 'intrinsic' effects of human actions."

Furthermore she says :—"There is a power *within* ourselves 'making for righteousness'; but it is not omnipotent, and is frequently held in check by adverse forces."

The other essays in this important volume comprise :—The "Philosophy of Thomas Carlyle," "The Brain Theory of Mind and Matter; or Hylo-Idealism,"

" Hylo-Idealism : the Creed of the Coming Day," " The
Principles of Sociology," and " Animal Automatism—
A Criticism of Dr. Huxley's Essays on 'Science and
Culture.'"

But to return to the narrative. Later on, during
the summer of 1889, in company with Mrs. Daniell,
Miss Naden visited the Paris Exhibition, which was
a source of much pleasure to them both.

The claims of sweet charity—that "voluntaryism,"
so incessantly urged by Mr. Herbert Spencer, as
opposed to the " State-aid compulsion," which he
everywhere as strongly deprecates—also appealed to
her sympathies; and shortly before her death she was,
as a member of the Working Ladies' Guild, in correspondence with Lady Mary Feilding (the founder of
the guild) with regard to taking the entire charge and
responsibility of the Campden Houses, a block of
houses on Campden Hill, arranged for the reception
of ladies of limited means. On April 1st of the year
above mentioned, she held a drawing-room meeting at
her house, in aid of the new Hospital for Women, in
Marylebone Road, which was largely attended, and at
which her friend, Mrs. Garrett Anderson, M.D.,
delivered an address on the subject of the hospital
and its relations to the training of medical women for
India. At the close of the meeting several hundred
pounds were obtained in aid of the funds. Miss
Naden was most generous in her private charities ;
poor ladies being a special subject of interest to her,
and she agreed with Mrs. Daniell, one day when they
were chatting over the subject together, that " she had

so many private cases to help that she had little money
to subscribe to public charities."

Progress, emancipation, and social reforms
naturally had a large share of Miss Naden's active
energies. She was a Liberal in politics, and canvassed
for Mr. G. Leveson-Gower (the present Member for
Stoke-upon-Trent), when he was an unsuccessful
candidate for Marylebone. She was a member of the
Denison Club, principally composed of members of
the Charity Organization Society, who met monthly to
discuss questions connected with the condition of the
poor. She was also a member of the Somerville Club
(only for women), and of the National Indian
Association, in which she took much interest after her
Indian tour, and attended several of its meetings and
conversaziones. She was also a member of the Norwood
Ladies' Debating Society, and at one meeting argued
against Miss Grover, who took the Socialist side.
Miss Naden was in favour of the extension of the
suffrage to women, and, under the auspices of the
Women's Liberal Association, gave a lecture at
Deptford, November 19th, 1889, on the subject, which
has been described by one of her audience as having
been delivered "in that matured and commanding
strain of oratory which only the very highest gifts could,
at her age, either impart or justify."

Miss Naden's last public appearance in Birmingham was at the Mason College, on Tuesday evening,
22nd October, 1889, on the occasion of the opening
meeting for the session of the Sociological Section, in
which she took such deep interest. With her usual

E

generously altruistic nature, she had some weeks before promptly complied with the request of the President that she would deliver an address as a preliminary to the subsequent exposition by her fellow-members of the first volume of Mr. Herbert Spencer's *Principles of Sociology.* The meeting was held in the large Examination Hall of the College, and the attendance, which included many ladies, was numerically and intellectually strong, numbering nearly a hundred. Among the audience were all the members of the Section, and some of the members of the other sections of the parent Society, a few of her old companions of College days, several of her near relatives and intimate friends, and three or four of the learned professors, her former teachers in the College. Her address was read in a remarkably clear and impressive voice—the intonation being so perfect that it penetrated into every corner of the hall—and was listened to with rapt attention during the period of upwards of an hour which it occupied in delivery. During the pauses, which naturally fell here and there, hearty and sympathetic applause was accorded. Her finely-cut and highly intellectual face never seemed so bright and earnest. Many friends remarked on her apparent good health and spirits, and that all traces of her Indian illness had disappeared. At the conclusion, a cordial vote of thanks to the able Sociologist for her valuable address, accompanied by a request that she would allow it to be printed, was moved by Mr. W. B. Grove, M.A., President of the Society, and seconded by Professor Tilden, D.Sc.,

F.R.S. In his subsequent remarks, the learned professor paid her the high compliment of saying that she had acted wisely in undertaking original work rather than striving for a degree—a compliment, we believe, that has rarely been paid before, except by Professor Michael Foster in the case of the late F. M. Balfour. Her staunch friend and former teacher, Professor Lapworth, LL.D., F.R.S., J. A. Langford, LL.D. (whose *Century of Birmingham Life* she had referred to in her address), and her old fellow-student, Mr. F. J. Cullis, F.G.S., the first president of the College Union Debating Society, also spoke in the warmest terms, and the motion was carried with acclamation.

The address—which was soon after published in the *Midland Naturalist*, and subsequently included by Dr. Lewins in his volume of her posthumous works, previously mentioned, but the proofs, alas! were never touched by the "vanished hand"—commenced with a plea in favour of the new science of Sociology, and a subsequent definition of the nature and scope of its aims and objects, with some account of the various complicated factors which regulate its inter-dependence and progress, together with comparative illustrations from primitive and other races, and, after a picture of a contrast between the Birmingham of the present day and that of one hundred and forty years ago, thus concluded :—

"A society like ours ought to find its ideal in that 'possible future social type,' which, in Mr. Spencer's words, 'will use the products of industry neither for maintaining a militant organization, nor exclusively for material aggrandisement, but will devote them to the carrying on of higher activities,—a type which, instead of believing that 'life is for work,' will hold the inverse belief that 'work is for life.'" These were the impressive last words spoken in Birmingham by Constance Naden.

It was a distinct triumph both for the author and the cause, and the memory of the meeting will for ever be treasured by those who had the privilege of being present. That the gifted lady herself appreciated her reception is confirmed by the following brief extract from a letter addressed to the President the next day:—"I felt rather overwhelmed last night, and am beginning to consider myself a sort of Solar Myth; but I did feel everyone's kindness very much. I am afraid I shall not be fit for the Saturday Excursion, but I suppose I need not decide till to-morrow. How many do you think were present last night? It was a much better audience than I expected." Happily for once, as we now see it—for it might have hastened her end—the indifferent weather prevailing at this time proved a blessing, for we abandoned our intended excursion to Sutton Coldfield, to the disappointment of many, as her friend, Dr. Showell Rogers, had promised to read an interesting paper, which, however, he afterwards gave at the Mason College. Miss Naden called on the writer of these lines for the last time, for a few minutes, on Friday, October 25th, and, although she did not utter a word of complaint, her intelligent face looked anæmic, anxious, and careworn, so very different from its radiant appearance only three nights before. Her energy, however, seemed unabated, and even at this time, so bravely did she bear up, that, with but little persuasion —which, however, was not attempted—she would have joined the contemplated excursion. Reference was made to her address, which was shortly to appear in the *Midland Naturalist*, and she expressed herself pleased at the notice of it in the day's *Daily Post*. Little thinking that we should never meet again, the writer bade a cordial good-bye to the cherished friend whom he saw no more.

As read by the light of subsequent events, how inexpressibly sad seems a passage in this address alluding to the incomplete knowledge of our own times :—"What are we ourselves, viewed as social units? Whither are we moving, and what is the curve of our line of progress? What is the goal towards which we are really working?—for it may be, and probably is, far other than that which we set before our imagination. Not possessing the solution of these enigmas, we cannot know the full sociological significance of our own day or of any previous day, since part of that significance lies in the unseen future. The future is, without doubt, as rigorously predetermined by past and present, as the nature of the harvest is predetermined by the nature of the seed that is sown. If we really knew the crop, we could both predict the harvest and could trace its past history from the formation of the ovule to the liberation of the seed when mature. No child of the

century can truly understand himself or his age, or
can solve the problems in which he himself is a
factor. If he could, he would be a child not of this
century, but of all centuries. As our knowledge
advances, and as our apprehension of principles
becomes more definite and coherent, we may learn to
distinguish many of the 'streams of tendency' which
flow around us or bear us onward; but the inter-
actions even of those which are seen are far too
complex to be worked out by the clearest intellect.
And we can never be certain that the most important
currents have not remained unobserved, just because
we are moving with their motion."

What happened after the Birmingham visit may
be briefly told. Symptoms of severe internal illness
were discovered, and, as the result of several medical
consultations, presided over by Sir Spencer Wells, an
operation was decided upon, and performed by Dr.
Lawson Tait, at her residence, 114, Park Street,
Grosvenor Square, on Thursday, the 5th December.
The public were then informed of the critical state
of the patient. For some little time it was hoped
that she would have sufficient vitality to recover, and
on the 18th December, only a few days before the
fatal termination of the illness, Mrs. Daniell wrote:—
"I am very happy to tell you that our dear friend is
now getting on very well. She is very weak, but I trust
that will soon be overcome by the kind care of Dr.
Grigg and nurses, and she is able to take a fair amount
of nourishment. We hope to-morrow to remove her
to another room." Sorrowful to say, the improvement

was not maintained, and, after a fainting fit, which occurred about eleven o'clock in the forenoon of Sunday, December 22nd, she became extremely weak, and on the following day, December 23rd—ere she had fully completed her thirty-second year, and retaining perfect consciousness—she gradually sank, and at a quarter to two o'clock in the morning quietly passed "to where beyond these voices there is peace."

Necessarily, her medical attendants are extremely reticent as to the details of her illness, but such as could be given strongly impress one with the extraordinary courage and powers of endurance she must have had. Practically, her illness had taken a fatal form as early as June or July, 1889, from which only an operation of the most desperate character afforded the slightest chance of relief. Yet, in spite of this delay, her marvellously placid temperament enabled her to pull through so as almost to make a recovery. So far indeed was this recovery effected that she was almost able to leave her sick-bed, and her sudden death could be entirely attributed to conditions which had arisen long antecedent to the operation.

Only so recently as the last meeting of the Sociological Section, held in the month of December, 1889, a resolution was passed congratulating Miss Naden on her progress towards convalescence, and on the first meeting in January following, when her death was announced, the Section recorded "the deep sense of regret at the irreparable loss which the cause of Evolution had sustained by the early death of their gifted friend and colleague, who for many years had advocated the doctrine of the Synthetic Philosophy with a genius, ability, and enthusiasm rarely equalled." At a meeting of the committee of the Central National Society for Women's Suffrage, held in London, in January last, presided over by Lady Sandhurst, the following resolution, upon the motion of Mrs. Ashton Dilke, seconded by Miss F. Pennington, was unanimously passed:— "That the committee have heard with profound regret of the death of Miss Constance Naden, who had evinced her warm interest in women's suffrage by entering the ranks of those who publicly advocate the question. They deplore the loss of one who, by her ability and zeal, would have done so much to advance the cause of women, and they would respectfully tender to the members of her family their most sincere sympathy."

A few words may be devoted to personal characteristics, which are very pleasant to dwell upon. It was impossible to be in Miss Naden's company without the unmistakable feeling that one was in the presence of a superior intelligence. To a stranger there appeared at first a kind of deep seriousness or natural shyness in the slim and fair unaffected girl, who from her youth and freshness seemed so little qualified to enter into recondite subjects, but this feeling was immediately dispelled when her bright smile showed sympathy with any matter of passing interest. And when her conversation warmed with enthusiasm, as it often did in discussions on the subject of evolution, one always felt that it was better to listen than to talk. In speaking, her voice, which was usually of high pitch—and had a slight natural peculiarity in the pronunciation of the letter " r," rather pleasing than otherwise—was remarkably clear, impressive, and penetrating, and she was equally confident either before a small or a large audience.

Her friend, Mrs. Daniell, describes her as "tall, slender, pale, with dark hair; a delicate, yet powerful face, with singularly clear blue-grey eyes. . . . She had especially small white hands, but was not at all fond of needlework. She used to write for some hours almost every morning, but was very fond of walking, and never failed to take out-door exercise once or twice every day, till told by her medical attendant, Dr. Grigg, that she must remain in the house." Mrs. Daniell, speaking of her before her fatal illness, also says:—"Every function, bodily and mental, seemed to be in just balance, so that she was never unduly elated by fortune, nor overwhelmingly depressed by misfortune, common to all mankind. It was the vigour and sound sanity of her brain which gave her this self-mastery, and to it she owed the ease with which she could pass from the lightest topics of daily life to the highest regions of abstruse thought, and *vice versâ*."

Music had little attraction for her, but her poems exhibit a skilled knowledge of the laws of rhythm. For gardening she had no taste, though so fond of flowers and botanical studies. Her sense of humour was decidedly keen. This came out sometimes in conversation, and is conspicuous in several of her poems, and occasionally appears in her prose writings. To her friends, her manner was undeviatingly kind, cordial, and affectionate. Her letters, in very dainty hand-writing, of which a few brief extracts have been given, were singularly frank and genial. Her fine and sweet temper was especially remarkable.

Mr. Naden, her father, thus writes :—" My dear daughter was a great admirer of energy and determination, and especially took an interest in the doings of her half-brother, George F. S. Naden, who, seeing no immediate field for his exertions here, wished to try what he could do abroad; accordingly he went to the State of Minnesota, U.S.A., and eventually became located in a sea-port on the Pacific coast, and proved very successful in his efforts. Constance corresponded with him, and asked what books he would like. The result was that she forwarded to him some treatises on geology and other books, selected, I believe, by Professor Lapworth. Her half-brother, Percy T. Naden, and her relative, Mr. A. D. Brooks, are named as executors in her will."

" It may be of interest to note "—says a valued correspondent—" that many years ago Miss Naden was taken by Dr. Lewins to visit his friends, the late Mr. and Mrs. Bray, and Miss Hennell, at Coventry. She submitted, not without some amusement, to a phrenological examination by Mr. Bray, who was much struck by the resemblance of her head to that of George Eliot. The only estimate of her character, from this external study of it, which I can remember, is ' strong

tenacity in friendship.' That this was true to a
remarkable degree, her many friends can testify ; while
her poem ' Friendship,' shows how high was her own
standard of its possibilities."

Miss Maude Michell, the beloved friend whom
I have already quoted, favours me with a few observa-
tions. She says:—"I should like to add my testimony
to that of Mrs. Daniell, that mental strain, at least as
far as study was concerned, bore no part in the development of the disease from which Miss Naden died.
Study was never an effort to her, but was as easy and
natural as novel reading is to most girls. During the
period in which most of her literary work was accomplished, *i.e.*, between 1881 and 1887, I saw her
constantly, and although a very considerable portion
of her time was spent daily at the Mason College, I
never once remember her confessing or showing the
least trace of strain from overwork. Indeed, she
did not even feel the necessity of a study, but wrote in
a room where she was subject to constant interruptions,
and where she was always ready to break off her train
of thought, to answer a question from Mrs. Woodhill,
who always sat with her, or to entirely set aside her
work to receive her friends."

"An important note in Miss Naden's character,"
continues the same friend, "is struck by a sentence
in her criticism of *John Ward, Preacher*. 'I believe'
(she says, in a letter dated September 12th, 1889)
'you will agree with me that Helen shows a
strange lack of perception in treating her husband's
views so lightly. She should have seen that to

him they were vital.' In this spirit she ever
regarded the opinions of those who differed from her,
when she was convinced that their aim was 'truth
at any cost.' Thus she writes, 'Don't let difference
of opinion make the *least* change in our friendship,'
and when time had proved that it could not do so,
'I always feel certain, with you, that our deepest
feelings are in sympathy. Without that, no agreement
of mere opinion is worth anything—as I have often
felt—and with it, even the interchange of thought
sometimes seems unnecessary; and yet it is good to
interchange thought, and to speak sometimes of what
is most sacred to us.' "

Mrs. F. T. S. Houghton, the other life-long friend
previously alluded to, also thus writes to me her
impressions:—"No one had a keener appreciation of
fun, or entered more readily into a frolic than Miss
Naden in her college days. She shared in all the
frivolities of the ladies' room—the afternoon teas, at
which

> The cups were every shape and size
> That chance or purpose could devise;
> But one and all the self-same hue,
> And that was like the maidens—*blue ;*—

and the *very* occasional gossip. In conversation *à deux*,
Miss Naden had a special charm. She not only gave
of her best, but extracted the best that was in one.
To talk to her was, indeed, to drink in inspiration;
to receive a letter from her brilliant, facile pen, was
to know a joy which falls to the lot of few. It is
difficult for one who has grown up with Miss Naden
from childhood, and known her primarily as a tenderly

affectionate and deeply sympathetic friend, to at all realise the impression of hardness and reserve which she is said to have sometimes produced upon strangers. Like George Eliot, she had the intellect of a man, but the heart of the most womanly of women, and though science and literature were much to her, love and friendship were infinitely more. What we have lost, whom she loved and who loved her, no words can say; the grief is still so recent that as yet we scarcely dare to gauge it."

And now there remains but the final scene to record. On Saturday, 28th December, 1889, under leaden-coloured skies, in a bitter north-east wind, and with "rime in the air, sucking the vital warmth out of every living thing," all that was mortal of the gifted poetess and philosopher was consigned to its resting place at the Old Cemetery, Warstone Lane, Birmingham, on the south side, and in the grave where repose the mother whom she never knew, and those " guardians true " who had watched her from her infant days

"With tenderest love and care."

The ceremony was singularly quiet and unostentatious, "bestowing peace for grief," the mourners being the father and other sorrowing relatives, together with her fellow-traveller and companion, Mrs. Daniell. A few friends beyond this sacred circle reverentially attended to pay a last tribute of respect to the beloved one for whose sterling work in the past they had such profound admiration, and of whose potentiality in the future they had formed a still higher estimate. They included Miss Charles, B.Sc., and Miss Edwards, B.A., on behalf of the lady students of the Mason College; and the following as principally representing the Sociological Section, namely:—Alfred Browett, W. B. Grove, M.A., Alfred Hayes, M.A., W. R. Hughes, F.L.S., W. Showell Rogers, LL.D., and Ernest C. Rogers, LL.D.

The solemn service of the Church of England for the burial of the dead was read by the Rev. W. E. Ivens, M.A., Vicar of St. James's, and as we mournfully left the deep open grave in the soft red sandstone, wherein were placed by loving hands wreaths of fresh green maiden-hair fern, intermingled with camellias and other white flowers, our thoughts turned to the bright spirit whose course had been so brief here, but who had nevertheless left her impress, as unconsciously foreshadowed in her ever-memorable lines in "The Pantheist's Song of Immortality"—

"Thou yet shalt leave thine own enduring token,
   For earth is not as though thou ne'er hadst been."

And so, in the closing words of that other lofty poem, the merits of which she was among the first to recognise,

"THE DEWDROP SLIPS INTO THE SHINING SEA."

WILLIAM R. HUGHES.

ADDITIONS.

PART III.

Der kühne Dichtertraum ist nicht verloren,
Er war zu eng, zu bleich :
Nur in des Menschen Seele wird geboren
Das Erd-und Himmelreich.

Das Ideal.

Constance Naden came to us in 1881. The story of her life at College would be short enough if a successful student-life could be summed up in a simple record of marks, classes or degrees. For the official testimony of the College Calendar shows that a very few class places and prizes taken, without obvious effort, in the course of some five years given to lecture room and laboratory, represent all there is to show to the outside world of the career of the most brilliant student the doors of Mason's College have yet admitted.

The proof that this estimate of her powers was shared by all her teachers is to be found in the roll of "Associates" of the College, where it may be seen that there is but one name to which is joined neither official title, nor University distinction, nor College diploma, in explanation or justification of its place in the list.* Professors, and students perhaps better than professors, knew how well that place had been

---

* This was written before the recent amplification of the list.

earned. In a burlesque report of an imaginary debate, printed in an early number of the College Magazine, she is referred to under the name " Hypatia," a sort of acknowledgment, perhaps not very appropriate, but still an intelligible acknowledgment of her position among her fellow-students.

From the first it was evident that, although she had no University examination in view, she had planned for herself a very definite and very complete course of study, with a very well defined purpose.

The study of philosophy, undertaken with the object of forming a true theory of life, requires that no branch of modern learning shall be omitted from the necessary preparatory course. Physical and biological science must both be explored. Miss Naden knew this, and accordingly, having determined to build high, she proceeded to lay her foundations deep, submitting to a very thorough drilling in the subject-matter of the sciences of physics, chemistry, botany, zoology, and geology. Then, as in one subject after another, she obtained command of the fundamental principles, with no mean acquaintance with its detail, she transferred her active intelligence, her keen reasoning faculty, and great powers of acquisition, to new ground. No inducements seemed sufficient to prevail upon her to become a mere scientific specialist. For her the absorbing questions seemed to be, What is man, whence and whither?

But though she came to gather for herself the elements of the synthetic philosophy which she thought to pursue as a life-work, she also gave freely of her time and talents to the social life of the College. For some time she served as editress of the Magazine, and was always, till she left England for the East, a chief contributor to its pages. In the first number of the first volume (1883) there is a sonnet of hers, "Hercules." The second number contains an article on "Scientific Idealism;" the next a paper on "Paracelsus."

The fourth number opens with an Editorial bearing her signature, in which a reply is framed to the question : "Is the increasing predominance of brain over muscle conducive to national welfare ?" And this reply so clearly indicates the habitually cheerful and healthy, as well as lucid, character of all her thought, that the final sentences, which contain the pith of the matter, may be appropriately quoted here. The increasing predominance *is* prejudicial "because it promotes excessive specialization, thus contracting the sphere of human sympathies, and widening the breach between the classes of which a nation is composed : and also because severe and continuous exercise of the brain tends to the disease and consequent atrophy of other parts of the body, inducing an unhealthy condition which must in time re-act upon the organ of mind. The heart, which is a muscle, will revenge itself upon the brain. A nation, which has forgotten how to enjoy, will soon forget how to think—and the sooner the better."

Here the fallacy—if there is one—lies in the assumption that there is a predominance of mind over muscle in modern civilised life, and that it is increasing.

The predominance is probably an assumption for which the justification seems to be that it is apparent chiefly among those classes of persons whose mode of life was most familiar to the writer.

These selections serve to show the habitually serious turn of her mind, while a couple of pages of verse, under the title "Scientific Wooing," in the third number, provide an example of her sprightly humour, of which other instances are scattered through the later numbers of our magazine, as well as in the published volumes of her poems. Unfortunately she was obliged to resign the editorship in December, 1884. The last act of what may be regarded as her student life was the composition of the essay on *Induction and Deduction*, for which the first award of the Heslop Gold Medal was made. Then came the journey to the East, her illness in India, and return home. Her friends hoped for the best, and looked forward with confidence to the ripening of that noble fruitage of which the spring-time of her life had given promise so abundant. This, however, was not to be. The treasure of this young and ardent life is spilled and wasted ; and for those of us who mourn her loss there is no consolation but the memory of the flower that lived but such a little day and then was seen no more.

WILLIAM A. TILDEN.

IV.

"Take the Godhead into your own Being,
And It abdicates its cosmic throne."
SCHILLER.

"The important question, What is the rule of Life? is lost out of the world."—BISHOP BUTLER.

A memoir of Miss Constance Naden, as Mr. Hughes and myself agree in thinking, which should ignore the scientific hylo-ideal, or automorphic principle, or synthesis underlying and suffusing her whole intellectual and ethical architectonic, would be like the tragedy of Hamlet *minus* its Protagonist.

I shall here state, in as few and clear words as possible, the *data* on the furthest rim of her horizon, which coloured and inspired all her utterances, in prose or rhyme ; premising that ever since leaving College she had bid adieu to poetry, and was concentrating all her powers for the composition of what she called her *magnum opus*, embodying these esoteric convictions, to which she became a convert while still in her early girlhood—a composition cut short by her premature death. Without this revelation of her inner life much, especially of her later poetry and prose, must be as enigmatical, and indeed incomprehensible, as Volapük. None of her readers, in its absence, will find it practicable to appreciate what the Germans term her

Weltanschauung, or world-scheme, as regards either the Macrocosm or the Microcosm of Man.

My chief difficulty in this exposition is the elementary *naiveté* and simplicity of the concept, or ideal, involved—the conclusion being more self-evident than any premises leading up to it which I could possibly frame—that conclusion being only common sense, and, indeed, *common-place* fact, proverbially grander and stranger than all fiction. Her own most explicit utterances of her esoteric faith or unfaith are contained in her essays on *The Brain Theory of Mind and Matter*, on *Hylo-idealism, the Creed of the Coming Day*, in her analysis of Carlyle's genius and of his *Spiritual Optics*, in her critique of Professor Huxley's *Essays on Culture*, in her tract *What is Religion?* and in her German poem, *Das Ideal*, at page 76 of her *Songs and Sonnets of Springtime*, not to mention passages, *passim*, in which, less explicitly, the same world-scheme may be read between the lines.* To these writings I beg to direct the attention of all serious students of her life-work solicitous to verify, at first hand, her settled opinions, aspirations, and convictions. All I can pretend to do in this synopsis is to indicate the nature of the *primum mobile*— at once Archimedean *fulcrum* and lever—by means of which she moves, and, indeed, evolves the universe —a principle based exclusively on well-established *data* of Physics, Physiology, and Moral Philosophy.

* See her posthumous volume, lately published by Bickers and Son, London, on *Induction and Deduction*, and other Essays.

From its far-reaching and exhaustive synthesis, it enables the "Writ of Positive Science" to run in regions, viz., those of Consciousness, in which, as the King's beyond the Highland line during the heritable jurisdiction of the Chiefs, it has hitherto been invalid. It heralds, therefore, a new departure in the provinces of Anthropology and Morals, clearing up *nugæ* that have hitherto ruinously hampered human insight and progress in its highest forms, while yet, as above stated, introducing no new element into the Sphinx-like problem. Its main coign of vantage, and that, now-a-days, itself quite a truism, is the coherent postulation, on simple and intelligible bases, of the fatuity of Absolute Knowledge, or true Ontology, or Causality, and the assured certainty, or entelechy, of its relativity or individuality—transcendence of which latter, corresponding with the impossibility of *exit* from what Lord Tennyson calls the "abysmal depths" of our personality, being manifestly a *reductio* not only *ad absurdum* but *ad impossibile.*

On this relational ordinance, therefore, unless we are prepared, like Tertullian, to believe just because it is impossible—each individual sentient Being— Beast or Man, Protozoon or Metazoon—must be relatively, *i.c.*, in itself, everything. "Thing," indeed, disappears altogether by transformation into conscious "think," no cognizance of object or *Non-Ego* being possible, until this mental (cerebral) transfiguration from non-egoistic externality into Subject-Egoity is consummated—a fact which is the key of the whole position, and the pivot upon which the mighty

question of Auto-Monism *versus* Dualism revolves.
This simple fact—simple as any conjuring trick when
once we have been initiated into its secret—is clearly
one with Kant's negation of the *Thing in itself*, or
Ding an sich. It is just as clearly *solidaire* with the
predicate that each individual sentient being, on the
relative or cerebro-ideal plane of ideation, *bien entendu*,
is the Maker or Creator, or Demiurge of the only
universe—abstract or concrete, visible or invisible, to
which it has access. *Quod supra, vel extra, nos* is
hylo-ideally, as the only "real reality" or factuality,
nihil ad nos. All students of ancient Greek wisdom
will recognise in this Neo-conceptualism the Gospel
of the Abderite sophist, Protagoras, in his own day,
though ultimately persecuted, like Phidias, Aspasia,
and Socrates, &c., if not literally crucified, for
Atheism—acclaimed like Christ—*Logos* and *Sophia;*
viz., that man, and, by implication, all other animals,
is to himself the measure and standard of all existence
and non-existence whatsoever—a formula utterly misunderstood by Plato, Bacon, G. H. Lewes, Grant
Allen, Proctor, Tyndall, and generally by most
special scientists, our contemporaries. This formula
unobscurely affirms that each individual Ego or Self is
the creator of its own world : *Faber mundi sui :* and that
there are as many worlds as there are *sensoria* to image
them—a different world being represented in, and by,
every individual brain ; constituting thus the veritable
apotheosis, canonization, or beatification of universal
Humanity, thus revealed as the Surrogate or Vicarius,
quite the Pope-King or White Czar, of an unknowable

Pseudo-Deity. Each sentient unit is thus monarchos and autocrat of all it surveys.

All impious presumption — a term Socrates applied to the astronomers of his own time—is eliminated from this Promethean and Titanic escalade —Heaven itself, like all things or nothings else, being but ideal, *i.e.*, a physiological state—an internal feeling, not an external "reality"—when we limit our faculties to phenomena or appearances. Indeed, the charge of presumption recoils on our gainsayers. A world-scheme based on the relativity or phenomenality (*by synecdoche*) of cognition is the really humble view, confining, as it does, human knowledge within its legitimate boundaries, but as a set-off—*the gain being incommensurably greater than the apparent loss* —making man supreme in that his only proper sphere. The real presumption clings thus to the Spiritualists, who seek to know, and assume to know, the unknowable and unverifiable. To search after the unsearchable, with which we have no real concern whatsoever, is self-evidently "vanity of vanities." It is like the futile efforts of the infant in arms to clutch the moon, or like attempting to jump down our own throat, out of our own skin, or to run from our own shadow. The real humility is to foreclose all pretensions to reach *veræ causæ* as entirely beyond the necessary limitations of the human mind (brain), and to rest content in the relativity of all *Gnosis*.

In modern times Bishop Berkeley's *Principles of Human Knowledge* is the *réchauffé* of the Abderite sophist's standpoint, as Spinoza's *Pantheism* of the later

Platonist Theocles, only the former, vitiated by the dual fallacy of the Absolute, from which Animism or Fetichism—a vicious relic from primeval medicine men—the Greek hylo-zoists who preceded Plato were exempt. Our christian and episcopal Protagoras enunciates his " Principle " thus : " Some truths there are so near and obvious to the mind that a man has only to open his eyes to see them. Such I take to be this most important one, that all the choir of Heaven and furniture of earth—in a word, all those bodies which compose this mighty frame of the world, have not any substance without a mind." This position, unlike Mr. Gladstone's "Rock of Holy Scripture," is impregnable. But, since out of our own cerebration we can never expatiate, that pseudo-alien mind can be no other than *our own*—the "unknown" Cause of Causes, therefore, which we blindly "seek after," and when hypothetically "found" assume to worship, being impossibly any other "making for righteousness," or the reverse, than the Pseudo-Deus-Homo, Ego, or Demiurge, our *Very Self of Very Self.*

In a tract published at 63, Fleet Street, in 1887, entitled *Humanism v. Theism,* I have dwelt more fully than I do here on the bearing of this auto-centric Solipsism on Eschatology. This tract consists, in addition to her essay on Hylo-Idealism, of extracts from letters addressed to Miss Naden, selected by herself, during the years 1878-80. They are prefaced by a note of her own stating that, after further verbal illustration, and after study of the exact and moral sciences, she became a convinced convert to

this world-scheme.   Berkeley's plea for Absolute
Idealism appeared in 1708, more than a hundred
and eighty years ago.   In that interval what
stupendous experiential developments, which at
bottom are all mental, have taken place.   Scotch
Moral Philosophy fiom Hutcheson to Hume and
Thomas Brown, of which Kantism is an offshoot,
German Rationalism dating from Lessing's Wolfen-
büttel Fragments (1774-78), the neology of modern
philological exegesis, and last in order, but first in
rank, the amazing evolution of the Positive Sciences,
not one of which existed in 1708, with the exception
of formal or ideal Newtonian Physics, and its appli-
cation to Astronomy.   Even that whilom Queen of
Sciences, now dethroned by "transcendental"
Anatomy, required the revision of Laplace and other
French Neo-Materialists, to get rid of the immaterial
extra-mundane Spiritism which vitiated its conclusions
in the domain of Philosophy.   No competent
astronomer, now-a-days, but must smile at Sir Isaac's
scholium about the *Ens Supremum*.   It is quite on a
par with Milton's mythology of Creation.   Medicine,
in Berkeley's age, and till the end of the eighteenth
century, was quite in the scholastic stage.   It only
entered the Positive phase under the genius of Xavier
Bichat, who, like the subject of this memorial sketch,
was cut off prematurely at the age of thirty-one years.
The Bishop's delusion as to the "virtue of tar water,"
which, during almost his entire lifetime, he extolled
as the "*infallible*" prophylactic and panacea for all
diseases of animals and vegetables, is proof sufficient

of the backwardness of the healing art, as well as of his own visionary disposition and complete incapacity for valid experimental research. *Mutatis mutandis,* like Dean Swift, he was, in Thackeray's words, " strangled by his own [clerical] bands."

All such minds are, as fetichists, *dualists,* who *must* hold animal Life to be the union of Soul and Body—a now quite antiquated and anti-scientific position, fundamentally one with the Archaism of Van Helmont, a Flemish nosologist, who died soon after Newton's birth. Now-a-days Monism—unity of body and mind—which defines sentient vitality as organic function, or organization in action, is the accredited creed of Science. That histological canon holds a separate soul or spirit, or *Noûs,* to be in Physiology, what Phlogiston or Caloric is in Chemistry and Physics, an imaginary factor or Nonentity. This thesis is well expressed by the late Sir Wm. Gull, M.D., in the sentences : " Until to-day [or rather yesterday] the theory that the living quality in us was due to a mysterious vital force [*i.e.,* immaterial spirit or principle] out of reach of science, pre-occupied the mind and stood in the way of observation and experiment. But now it has become the immovable standpoint of Physiology that a living creature is dependent for all its bodily functions upon the forces of inorganic matter ; or in other words, that our corporeal life is but the operation of material atoms and material forces within the reach of experimental enquiry."

Indeed, how can this be any longer a question, since the solidarity of the organic and inorganic was

set at rest by Wöhler's transmutation of the one into
the other by his artificial manufacture in the laboratory
of the organic product *Urea* from inorganic ones,
more than sixty years ago (1828)? So that now-a-
days organic chemistry is only that of the carbon
compounds. One step further, but that an epoch-
making, all-shattering one, reversing past and present
authoritative notions of human Ethics and Practice,
Miss Naden takes, when she resolves Hylozoism into
Hylo-idealism, of which the somatic Self is centre,
radius, and periphery. As must be the case if all our
knowledge be only an Autopsy, or Self-inspection—a
thought-world and thought being an alias of cerebration,
as impossible of vicarious or altruistic performance as
sleep or alimentation. The mere affirmation that the
Brain is *sensifacient*, or sense and mind creating, solves
the whole immemorial problem, which in all ages and
climes has maddened the hitherto only semi-rational
family of Man in doubt whether to deem himself a
God or Beast. Most seem quite content with being
the latter or worse. And until the human race can
be made to realise, and act upon the fact, that each of
its units is its own measure and standard no progress
worth the name, but only processes of alternate action
and reaction, can, in the way of Self- and world-
reformation, come to pass. Wanting this criterion of
truth and untruth, the extension of Luther's plea
for Private (individual) Judgment and liberty of
conscience, human nature must remain indefinitely
what Pope describes in the second epistle of his *Essay*

on Man, from the line "Know then thyself, presume not God to scan," to the couplet :

> " Sole Judge of Truth, in endless error hurl'd,
> The glory, jest, and riddle of the world."

Make "thing" only think or idea—an Ideal Pope vigorously and virulently combats and denounces in the 4th Book of the *Dunciad*—and the whole standing problem, usually pronounced insoluble, including the origin of "Evil," Determinism and Indeterminism, etc., is disentangled at one blow, like the Gordian Knot by the sword of the Macedonian conqueror. "Our Universe," writes Miss Naden, at page 10 of *Humanism v. Theism*, in one of many passages to the same effect throughout her writings, "is made up of sensations [or states of consciousness]. For even thought is but the special sense of the cerebral cortex, and beyond sensation we cannot pass. Even *Hyle*, the substance, the Unknowable, if you will, must be defined in terms of thought. * * Practically we may say of Self, as Paul of Christ : In it are all things created in the Heavens and upon Earth, things visible and things invisible ; all things have been created by it, and Self is before all things, and in self all things consist." Of course this is the Gospel of Selfism, far as the poles asunder from vulgar selfishness and Egotism. Lord Byron hails Berkeley's theory as a "sublime discovery," from its making the Universe universal Egotism, or rather Egoism. And the above quotation from Miss Naden converts this speculative dream into a sober, scientific excogitation not possible in his age. It quite corresponds with Sir Humphry Davy's ejaculations during the orgasm induced by Nitrous Oxide Gas : "Nothing exists but thoughts. The Universe is composed of impressions, ideas, pleasures, and pains." And when, quite restored to his normal condition, he describes himself as "by degrees losing all connection with *external* things, and as existing in a world of newly connected and newly modified ideas, and as seeming a new and sublime being, newly created." The Stoic and Christian Palingenesia, Pentecostal descent of the Paraclete, and all analogous raptures or *En*stases of Saints and Martyrs, "raising their longing eyes on high as though it were a bliss to die," can be nothing else than this hyperneurotic condition of the supreme nerve centres, and therefore a natural physiological phenomenon. The ecstatic or enstatic rhapsody of the emancipated Baccalaureus in Part II. of Goethe's *Faust*, translated by Miss Naden at page 173 of her *Modern Apostle*, and the quasi-divine vision of her Modern Apostle himself, on which she—through the medium of Ella—throws cold water, to say nothing of Calenture, Mirage of the Desert, and other cognate physiological states, are all instances of the same cerebro-cosmic exaltations, and Mount Tabor-like transfigurations.

Fichte's announcement at the close of one of his lectures at Jena, "Gentlemen, to-morrow I shall create God," and Schiller's lines in his *Life and the Ideal*, "With Man's resistance [to Reason] vanishes also the Majesty of God," all bear witness to the fact that percepts and concepts—emanations of the Self—form our entire universe. So that, instead of being the offspring in the domain of Consciousness, outside which is *taboo*, we really are the Parent of Deity.

On that neo-nominalist world-scheme—a view thoroughly verified by the records of all Religions from Serpent Worship to Jehovah, Jove, or Lord Jesus—Divinities are made in the image of their worshippers, not *vice versâ*. Autocentric Solipsism is well illustrated by the Brahman saying that "Brahm looking round can see nothing but himself;" or, to come nearer home, by the inscription on the monument of Sir Ch. Wren, in St. Paul's Cathedral, " *Si monumentum quæris circumspice ;*" or by what ought to have been the answer of the Neo-Materialist savants to Napoleon on the passage to Egypt, when he extended his arm to the Orient Stars, and fancied to foil them by asking who made all that. The real answer, on this plane of thought, ought to have been : "*Yourself. What you see is a vision of your own.*" Later in life he objected to Laplace's exclusion of Divinity from his system, to which the great geometer replied, differing thus *in toto* from Newton : "I have no need for that supposition."

I hope I have now made the philosophical esoterism of Miss Naden intelligible to all—never numerous, especially in un-ideal England—serious enquirers. It may all be summed up in the postulate that perception and conception, or, in one word, Thought or Idea, is an organic function, which, like all other natural offices, every one must perform for himself. To him, or her, who realises this necessity, the whole burden of my exposition is clear. *Egomet ipse* must be the universal "I am." When Bacon blames men for spinning webs, like spiders, out of their own entrails, he failed utterly to see through the problem. Man can do nothing else. The cerebral cortex is a *viscus*, and out of it proceed the issues of life and death, or what is the same, our consciousness of the former, of which the latter is only the privative. To myself the above canon covers the whole position. But, before closing, I may append additional concrete anatomical evidence, extracted from Dr. R. A. Lundie's recent contributions to the more recondite optical Anatomy, under the article "Eye," in Chambers's Encyclopædia, or Dictionary of Universal Knowledge. In that enlightened, and up to date monograph, Dr. Lundie writes: "In vision we do not look outwards towards the object, but inwards only, towards the object as mirrored [*i.e.*, manufactured] at the base of our own eye; the essential factors of vision—the rods and cones of the bacillary layer of the retina or Jacob's membrane, which are present by millions, being thus turned *away* from the light." This seems a perfect physical proof that the quasi-outer, or objective world, so far as we can or need see, is only an individual and subjective image of what Locke calls "*I know not what*," formed at the bottom of our own optical apparatus. I quote Chambers's Cyclopædia as a popular and accessible work of reference. The same morphological proof of automorphic Monism is more fully elaborated in Sir John Lubbock's *Senses of Animals* (International Scientific Series), and in other recent handbooks

G

dealing with this crucial problem. The reflected image on the retina, *corrected by the "Mind,"* points the same moral, that all we see is but an Autopsy. Kepler's *Supplement to Vitellio* is no satisfactory *rationale* of the puzzle; no "explanation" of an ultimate fact being possible or necessary. It is entirely *ultra vires rationis (cerebri)*, and therefore,. in sound science, and sober sense, quite out of court.

To scientific realism, in the supreme regions of thought and life, Lucretius' verdict, condemnatory of religion, is thus evidently equally applicable. Descartes' formula, *Cogito ergo sum* should only run *Cogito = sum.* Being and Thought, as highest mode of consciousness, are parallelisms. *Mens sana in corpore sano* should, in like manner, read *Corpus sanum = Mens sana.*

R. LEWINS.

NOTE.—It may not be unprofitable or un-interesting here to record the contemptuous and intolerant view that great literary Leviathan, Mr. Thomas Carlyle, took of the auto-cosmic principle at the root of Miss Naden's " Brain Theorem of Mind and Matter." On January 21st, 1870, of his Journal (page 388, Vol. II.), History of his Life in London, from 1835 to 1881, by Mr. Froude, we read as follows: " It is notable how Atheism spreads among us in these times. [Huxley's] protoplasm (unpleasant doctrine, that we are all, soul and body, made of a kind of blubber, found in nettles, among other organisms,) appears to be delightful to many, and is raising a great crop of atheistic *speech* on the shallower side of English spiritualism at present. One [Lewins], an army surgeon, has continued writing to me on these subjects from all quarters of the world, of which, after the first two or three, which indicated an insane vanity, as of a stupid cracked man, and a dull impiety as of a brute, I have never read beyond the opening word or two, and then the signature, as prologue to immediate fire; every one of which, nevertheless, gives one a moment of pain, of ghastly disgust and loathing pity, if it be not anger too, at this poor [Lewins] and his life.

"Yesterday there came a pamphlet, published at Lewes, by some moral philosopher, there called Julian, which, on looking into it, I find to be a hallelujah on the advent and discovery of Atheism ; and in particular, a crowning—with cabbage, or I know not what—of this very [Lewins]. The real joy of Julian was what surprised me—sincere joy you would have said—like the shout [howl] of a hyæna on finding that the whole universe was actually carrion. In about seven minutes my great Julian was torn in two, and lying in the place fit for him."

This forcible diatribe of the prose poet well illustrates the antithesis between Poesy and Science, which latter eliminates all mysticism from things, and, as in Hylo-idealism finally, on physiological grounds unifies object and the subject self. It recalls the dialectics of Socrates, who, when in prison, wrote pæans to Apollo and Diana, and who labelled the astronomers and other Hylo-zoists of his day as "impious madmen." And still more Dr. Johnson, in his scurrilous attitude towards Hume, Adam Smith, and Scotch Philosophy generally. As also in his absurd notion that he had "vanquished Berkeley," not exactly " with a grin," but "by a kick." Yet so it is ever in ages of progress and evolution. The boundary of the brain range of to-day becomes the truism of to-morrow; and yet the earlier generation cannot transcend their own limitations so as to enter into the borders of the promised land, but die in the arid wilderness. Carlyle's scorn and nausea of the Synthetic Philosophy, a wider world-scheme than either Kantism or Comtism, is notorious. Like Hylo-idealism, it seemed to his anti-scientific purview mere idiotism and iniquity ; as indeed did the critical system of the great Scoto-German, Kant.

New ideals rarely come to men above forty, as William Harvey recorded in the case of the circulation of the blood, and, alas, illustrated in his own person, by his persistent denial of Aselli's demonstration of the absorbent lacteal system.

R. L.

APPENDIX.

APPENDIX.

LETTER FROM MR. HERBERT SPENCER TO DR. LEWINS.

FAIRFIELD,
PEWSEY, WILTSHIRE,
June 10th, 1890.

DEAR SIR,

Before I received your letter of the 8th inst., I was about to write expressing my thanks for the copy ·you have kindly sent me of Miss Naden's *Induction and Deduction and other Essays.* Already I had formed a high estimate of her intellect and character, and now perusal of some parts of the volume you have sent me has greatly raised this estimate. Very generally, receptivity and originality are not associated; but in her mind they appear to have been equally great. I can think of no woman, save "George Eliot," in whom there has been this union of high philosophical capacity with extensive acquisition. Unquestionably her subtle intelligence would have done much in furtherance of rational thought; and her death has entailed a serious loss.

While I say this, however, I cannot let pass the occasion for remarking that in her case, as in other cases, the mental powers so highly developed in a woman are in some measure abnormal, and involve a physiological cost which the feminine organization will not bear without injury more or less profound.

I am glad to hear that you propose to publish another series of her Essays, and am quite willing that you should, if you wish, include in it the foregoing expression of my admiration.

I am, dear Sir,

Faithfully yours,

HERBERT SPENCER.

R. LEWINS, ESQ., M.D.

In a letter addressed to me, dated 17th August, 1890, Mr. Herbert Spencer desired that the following note from the Appendix to the *Study of Sociology* might be appended to his previous letter, in further explanation of the question raised therein, and in reply to subsequent criticism :—

"Perhaps, however, the most serious error made in drawing these comparisons [between the powers of men and women] is that of overlooking the limit of *normal* capacity. Either sex under special stimulations is capable of manifesting powers ordinarily shown only by the other; but we are not to consider the deviations so caused as affording proper measures. Thus, to take an extreme case, the mammæ of men will, under special excitation, yield milk : there are various cases of gynæcomasty on record, and in famines, infants whose mothers have died, have been thus saved. But this ability to yield milk which, when exercised, must be at the cost of masculine strength, we do not count among masculine attributes. Similarly, under special discipline the feminine intellect will yield products higher than the intellects of most men can yield.

But we are not to count this productivity as truly feminine if it entails decreased fulfilment of the maternal functions. Only that mental energy is normally feminine, which can co-exist with the production and nursing of the due number of healthy children. Obviously a power of mind which, if general among the women of a society, would entail disappearance of the society, is a power not to be included in an estimate of the feminine nature as compared with the masculine."

The implication pointed to by Mr. Spencer's letter, above quoted, is that in cases where the feminine intellect, under high pressure, is made to vie with the masculine in power, the physical tax tells primarily on the reproductive system, and, by partial arrest of its functions, tends to cause derangements.

W. R. H.

HERALD PRESS, BIRM.

www.ingramcontent.com/pod-product-compliance
Lightning Source LLC
Chambersburg PA
CBHW032146010726
47493CB00008BA/2597